KATA, THE IRON THORN

Thank you, Evan + Bonnie for All of your support throughout the years!!

ONE LOVE!!

Teddy Lee Barrett

KATA, THE IRON THORN

An Original Novelized Screenplay

TERRY LEE BARRETT

Kata: the Iron Thorn

Copyright registration number: PAU 3-704-608

Effective October 15, 2013

The Writers Guild of America East registration number: 1249554

Date: February 19, 2013

ISBN: 978-0-578-78559-2

To my Mom, Theodora, and my Dad, Dr. Leonard,
I've tried to do you proud with my feet on the ground
and my head in the clouds.

CONTENTS

THANK YOU

Dr. Leonard E. Barrett Sr.; Theodora Jackson-Barrett; Lyrata and Leonard E. Barrett Jr.; all Barrett and Jackson and Wells families; Georgie Woods; Java Immanuel; Franz Ace; George and Mark Burnett; Nobert G. Bain; Melanie Hughes; Emily Frelick and the Frelick family; Lynell Wilcha; Kathy Sledge; Maria Pandolfi; Dr. Carole Boyce Davies; Christopher Chaplin; Donahue Bailey; Barbara Wilson; Carlene B. Welles; Team Jamaica Bickle; Dr. Karren Dunkley; Kesi Gibson; Aubrey Campbell; Miranda Alexander; Yusufu Bryant; Duane Clemmer; Phil Graci; Carlos A. Ortiz; David Hahn; Tyler James; Marja Kaisla; Will Reed; Bob Lott; Maurice Browne; Jerry Wells; DJ Roger Culture; DJ Ross and DJ Lady Love; Timi Tanzania; Bernard M. Resnick; Louis Nathan; Bobbi Booker; Jennifer Lynn; Dr. Sheena C. Howard; Laurent and Danielle Bass; Jim Graham; Jeff "Mr. Trombone" Bradshaw; Fran Conner; Whitney Star; Justin Manne; George Polgar; Tyler Ward; Lance Silver; Stuart Harding; Kimberly D. Williams; Abington High School class of '74; Temple University; WHAT AM; WDAS FM; WRTI FM; WKDU FM; WMMR FM; the Inna Sense Reggae Band; Katmandu; Elite Authors; Old City Coffee; Jefferson Hospital; Brandywine Management; Old City T-Shirts; The Crew at Harry's Shop

FOREWORD

Kata, the Iron Thorn will do for the Caribbean what the Black Panther movie of 2018 did: igniting world interest in stories set in the African diaspora. This engaging narrative weaves together slavery and piracy, myth and legend, geography and science, love and intrigue—with surprising twists revealed.

The story incorporates the history of piracy and African enslavement on tropical shores. Kata is the African warrior king who fought against subordination, and as the story develops, we see him manifesting beyond the myth into an actual presence.

Well documented is the destruction of an old city called Port Royal, a pirate haven, from a massive earthquake in 1692. Buried there is a great deal of ill-gotten wealth. So there is an absolute reality to a narrative of piracy set in Jamaica.

But fast-forward to today. Kata Cove is where the main character is from and is the site of the action in which a son must reveal the family history of an ancestor with supernatural powers.

Thus, in this story, we are provided with a range of disappearances and reappearances, flashbacks that bring the past into the present, witches who can use current technology like cell phones, and a still-angry warrior king ancestor who must, in the end, find reconciliation and peace.

In many ways, Kata, the Iron Thorn is also a contemporary story that provides the experience of a young man who returns to the modern Caribbean with schoolchildren, Reggae music, Jamaican food, and celebration.

It is definitely about recovery and the putting back together of family history, a "re-membering," as Toni Morrison refers to this process. Somebody said recently that people of African descent in the Americas are hardwired to do family recovery, given the deliberate separations that

Africans in the diaspora have experienced. This is the kind of context that provides us with the still-iconic *Roots* and provides the ongoing discussion every time a film that reclaims some aspect of the past for good or ill is presented.

Many audience possibilities are envisaged with *Kata, the Iron Thorn*, applicable to different viewing communities. There is an obvious transferal to the young adult audience in the *Harry Potter* types of films. There is a large Caribbean and African international viewing public awaiting this kind of novel and movie. But as with *Pirates of the Caribbean* and a variety of action films, we are presented with an opportunity to impact even larger audiences.

My recent work on *Caribbean Spaces* (2013) has described Caribbean culture's internationalizing with entertainers like Rihanna moving into mainstream representations in various media. It seems that we are right at the cusp of advancing Caribbean literary and film material with an appeal to larger communities in much the same way as Bob Marley had a similar appeal to an international community. *Kata, the Iron Thorn* presents filmic innovation, which will provide the kind of far-reaching impact that is desired.

—Dr. Carole Boyce Davies

Dr. Carole Boyce Davies is a professor of English and Africana studies at Cornell University and a renowned author.

Chapter 1:

BACK TO JAMAICA

Our spooky adventure begins with an aerial view of Philadelphia, Pennsylvania, the huge William Penn Statue on top of City Hall, the Art Museum's "Rocky Steps," Independence Hall and the Liberty Bell, and an apartment building on a cobblestone street in the Old City neighborhood.

Disc jockey Terry Lee Barrett (a.k.a. DJ Terry Love), who now just wanted to be referred to as T. L., was heading to Jamaica to do battle with an obeah witch queen (a.k.a. a witch and other horrid characters), yet he didn't have a clue. T. L. was a true-to-life, sun-and-surf lover turned night owl. T. L. spent twelve years becoming a hotshot DJ at one of the trendiest clubs on the Philly waterfront. For Terry, young and on fire, daylight could not have come fast enough.

On this day, through the window into his bedroom, the sun was shining, just as he imagined. He was packing a suitcase and backpack with only the bare necessities like a few good pairs of beach shorts. T. L. started dancing as his favorite reggae video came on TV. The dancers in the video were real pros, and he tried to imitate their moves.

Looking for his keys on his crowded desk, he picked up an old flyer that read, "Reggae Night with DJ Terry Love and the Inna Sense Reggae Band Every Sunday Night." There was a picture of DJ Terry Love in an outdoor

DJ booth, wearing headphones and smiling ear-to-ear, on it. Those were the glory days, he thought to himself, when he was the DJ at the Katmandu Nightclub and Marina on the nearby Delaware River. Katmandu no longer existed, but it once had been a reggae and world music hotspot and the place T. L. deejayed for twelve delightful years. He tossed the flyer across the room, but it somehow would magically end up in his backpack.

He was now moving on with his career and opening his own club in Philly and hoped it would be as popular. He had countless meetings on setting up the club but had to take a sudden break from that routine, as he was called to Jamaica by his uncle Wilvo to claim the rights to his late father's historical house and land. His father was the late world-renowned Jamaican anthropologist the Reverend Dr. Leonard E. Barrett Sr., author and former professor at Temple University in Philly and other higher learning institutions.

His late mother, Theodora Jackson-Barrett, had been a journalist and the best mother of all time. She had been born in nearby Reading, Pennsylvania. Terry had lost both of his beloved parents from natural causes. His parents had met when his father attended Albright College there many years ago. After Dr. Barrett graduated from Albright, he moved back to Jamaica, where T. L. was born. Now, as the Barrett estate executor, Terry was doing his best to keep their legacy in order. Terry always felt that he didn't quite live up to his parents' expectations, being a DJ and all. However, he was having so much fun that he didn't have much time to dwell on it.

He hadn't been back to Jamaica in years. He had been born there but raised in Philly, which made him feel incredibly uncomfortable, as he didn't speak with a Jamaican accent. It was usually hard to persuade some Jamaicans or people in Philly that he was a Jamaican. When he would tell people that he was born in Jamaica, some people couldn't wait to refer to him as a "Jafaken." It was a little like being culturally homeless when, on the one hand, you can't talk like a Jamaican, and on the other hand, it's never good to speak like Rocky.

He decided to change his DJ name from "DJ Terry Love" to "DJ T. L." When he came up with the name Terry Love, he wanted to have a throwback name evoking the cool hippie era. Now it was time to lose that image. He felt the title DJ T. L. was less flowery and more Philly tough. Plus, people accused him of taking the Love handle from the Roots' celeb drummer Quest Love. But he knew that nothing could be further from the truth. After all, he had been known as Terry Love before Quest Love showed up on the global stage. If anything, he thought Quest might have taken it from him. Yep, he figured Quest possibly came to his incredibly popular reggae nights, noticed the name "Love," and ripped it off.

Terry Lee loved living in his Old City Philly neighborhood. However, heading back to Jamaica was always fascinating for the love of the music, the jerk chicken and all the rest of the glorious food, the sand, and the incredibly warm blue waters of the Caribbean Sea.

T. L. got a phone call; it was the cab driver outside. He trotted out of the apartment building with his suitcase and backpack, wearing his new green linen island-style shirt and pants, a green mesh fedora hat, a stainless-steel diving watch, and green slip-on loafers. He was lookin' good, like a superfly Philly DJ should. He got into the cab. "Philadelphia International Airport, right?" the cab driver asked.

"You know it, brother! I'm going on a little vacation." T. L. grinned.

"Yeah, where you goin'?" the cab driver asked.

"To Jamaica, mon!" T. L. said in his bad Jamaican accent.

"You lucky, brother!" the cab driver said.

Next thing you know, T. L. was sleeping on the Caribbean Air jet and was on his way. He was in his seat and dreaming. In his dream, a Jamaican woman (Empress Iyadola) floated up to him, wearing a tiara of red hibiscus flowers and an ornate necklace and wristband and holding a golden cow horn (the Magic Golden Abeng). Then, he smelled something very funky. T. L. turned to his left and was frightened by the appearance of an undead warrior seated next to him. The undead warrior was wearing a gold African kings crown, gold earrings, a kente-cloth vest, a gold ring on each of his fingers and thumbs, and white pantaloons, clutching a large rugged-looking sword, and he was in his bare feet. This was the undead Kata.

Kata raised his fists forward, thumbs up in the air. Kata spoke: "Ya gwan ta learn ta respeck di Kata, mon! Kata, nyaka! Kata, nyaka! Nyaka-nyaka!" Kata stood and faced the jet's passengers and yelled, "Forevah farward! Woyo! Woyo! Wo, wo!" The jet passengers stood and gave Kata lively forward-pointing, thumbs-up signs and yelled, "Forever forward! Woyo! Woyo! Wo, wo!" The passengers gave each other thumbs-up signs and fist bumps and cheers. Kata lowered his fist and thumb toward T. L.'s face, anticipating a fist-and-thumb bump from him.

T. L. woke up in a sweat. The jet was pin-drop quiet, other than the murmur of the jet engines. He slowly and reluctantly looked to his left. He was relieved to see a beautiful woman fast asleep. He noticed that she had exceptionally long legs and big but manicured feet. He noticed a supermodel magazine on her lap, and she was on the cover. The headline on the magazine cover read, "Wow, It's Greta!" Greta woke up and said in a German accent, "What?"

T. L. was shocked. "Oh, I'm sorry! Did I wake you?"

"You want my autograph?" replied Greta. Greta signed her name on the magazine. "Here, take it!" she demanded. Greta turned and went back to sleep. He put the magazine in his backpack.

Jason Clarke, a Jamaican who lived in Philly, walked up to him and gushed, "Respect, DJ Terry Love! Di J-I-C! Di Jamerican in Charge! Di reggae soooul brodda! Reggae rockin', dancehall droppin', soca nonstoppin', and world music boomshockalockan! What's up, you going home, mon? Back to Jamaica?"

Wearily, T. L. responded, "Hey, Jason Clarke. Yeah. Oh, man, I had a horrible nightmare! Oh, I think I'm going to be sick."

Jason was concerned. "You look like you saw a duppy ghost, mon, a spirit! What was di nightmare about?"

"It was like an undeadlike guy with a huge sword. Uh." T. L. fretted.

"An undead-like guy wit a huge sword or a Jamaican undead-like guy wit a huge sword?" Jason queried.

"What's the difference? It scared me half to death!" T. L. lamented.

"Well, a Jamaican undead-like guy wit a massive sword would be referred to as a duppy ghost. Spelled D-U-P-P-Y. A Jamaican duppy ghost is a shape-shifting spirit dat can take on human or animal form. There's no scarier ting in di world den a Jamaican duppy ghost spirit! It can talk, cook, strike you down, cause you to drown yourself—" Jason said.

"OK, Jason! Thank you for all that great information!" T. L. interrupted.

"No problem, mon!" Jason assured him.

"You know about my father, the Reverend Dr. Leonard Barrett Sr.?"

"Of course, he was a famous—" Jason said.

"Anthropologist. He passed away ten years ago," T. L. stated.

Jason acknowledged him. "Yeah, I know. I was sorry to hear dat, mon. He wrote di book on di Rastafarians, right? Everybody in my family read dat book."

"Well, I found out he also wrote another book," T. L. announced.

"Yeah, what about?" Jason asked.

"About witchcraft in Jamaica," T. L. said. T. L. handed Jason his father's book entitled *The Sun and the Drum: Witchcraft in Jamaica*.

Jason exclaimed, "Wow! Really?"

"My uncle Wilvo sent me that book. He has demanded that I speak on my father's behalf at a book fair in Kata Cove, Jamaica, today. He bought the plane tickets, got me free room and board—everything," T. L. informed him.

Jason remembered. "Kata Cove? Isn't dat where di famous pirate and duppy ghost fighter is from?" Jason posed like he was Superman giving a lively thumbs-up sign. "Kata, di Iron Thorn!!" Jason lowered his fist and thumb toward T. L.'s face, looking for a fist-and-thumb bump from him.

T. L. was bewildered. "Who? I had in no way heard of Kata Cove until my uncle Wilvo mentioned it a few weeks ago. It turns out it's where my father and I were born. All this time, I thought he and I were born in Kingston. Kata Cove is an hour's ride away in some far-off place. I mean, I'm honored, but I'm not a professor, and I certainly don't know anything about witchcraft."

"Neither do I." Jason scoffed. Jason looked at a page in the book of a gruesome rolling calf duppy ghost with fire coming out of its nose. Jason quickly handed him the book back. "You keep it! You'll probably need it. So, Mr. Big-Time Disc Jockey, I hear you're deejaying at a new club in Philly?"

"Yeah, it's called Club Bank. I am the O-A-D-J-I-C," T. L. said.

"What does dat mean?" Jason chuckled.

"It means 'owner and disc jockey in charge'! No reggae nights, unfortunately," T. L. clarified.

"No? Why not?" Jason wondered.

"Well, the club is downtown on Rittenhouse Square, and I'm trying to change my image a little. Yes, I was born in Jamaica, but everyone knows I was raised in Philly. I don't even speak with a Jamaican accent, and you know what happens when I try," T. L. lamented.

"Yeah, don't even try, Terry!" Jason giggled.

"It's time for me to be a Philly guy. That means rap, soul, rock, and dance music. Some reggae, but that's it," T. L. said.

"Are you kiddin' me? But like you always say, 'I was born in Kingston, Jamaica, and raised in Philadelphia, P-A...I'm your reggae soul brodda from around da way!' " Jason was complimenting him.

"No more Terry Love, di reggae soouul brodda from around da way! OK? It's T. L. now! Love's got nothin' to do with it! I got to make my money, man!" T. L. complained.

Jason lectured Terry. "Bwoy, reggae is your roots, your history, Terry Lee Barrett! 'A people without the knowledge of their history, origin, and culture is like a tree without roots.' Marcus Garvey said dat. You tryin' to forget dat? 'Ya gwan learn to respeck, mon.' Your Kata said dat! I was about to tell you that I graduated from the Philly DJ School. I was first in my class as a reggae DJ. I wanted to be a reggae DJ because of you. Keep di faith, Terry Love."

Jason walked away upset. An old pirate map of Kata Cove fell out of *The Sun and the Drum* book onto T. L.'s lap. A flight attendant announced, "We hope you have enjoyed your flight from Philadelphia to Montego Bay, Jamaica. We will be landing in Montego Bay shortly."

Chapter 2:

ARRIVING IN JAMAICA

A BMW limo pulled up to the passenger pickup area at the Montego Bay airport. A huge native Jamaican, a Taino, was the chauffeur. The original human inhabitants of Jamaica were known as the Taino people. At the time of European contact in the late fifteenth century, they were the principal inhabitants of most of Jamaica, Puerto Rico, Cuba, the Dominican Republic, and Haiti. In the seventeenth century, many Africans were enslaved and brought to Jamaica to work in the sugar cane fields on plantations. Today, most of the people that live in Jamaica are of African descent, and it is a very proud, successful, and independent island nation. Nicknames are popular in Jamaica, and they often describe either what you look like or what you are. This chauffeur's real name was David Rodriguez, but his nickname was what he was: "Taino." His chauffeur's suit was a size too small for his substantial six-foot-five frame. Taino helped T. L.'s uncle Wilvo out of the limo. The seventy-year-old—wearing an old-school wide-lapeled suit with gray-and-blue pinstripes and a matching cap—wiped away tears.

"Taino, do you see him yet?" Uncle Wilvo asked.

"Not yet, Uncle Wilvo," Taino responded. A poor, shirtless ten-year-old kid wearing shorts and no shoes hobbled up to Taino and pointed to a mango tree. "Hey, Taino, pick a mango for mi from di tree dayah?" the kid pleaded.

Taino scolded, "Bwoy, what you take mi for, your personal giraffe? Gwan, get a mango for yaself, ana one for mi too."

"Mi serious, Taino! Mi damage mi leg an' cyan't climb di tree, and mi nah eat nottin' all day!" the kid begged.

Taino handed the kid a few coins and pointed to a parrot in the tree. "Here, bwoy! Ya, see dat parrot in di tree? Ya, tell him Taino said hello! Cause mi know you can climb di tree! So now gwan!" The little kid laughed and then ran over to the tree. Taino looked closely at the strange, gangly looking parrot. It had large, spooky green eyes and ruffled feathers and appeared to be staring at him.

T. L. walked out of the Montego Bay terminal door and saw Taino with his sign. He waved to Taino. "I'm Terry Lee Barrett," T. L. yelled.

"Respect, bredren! Respect." Taino approved. Uncle Wilvo fell over, and T. L. and Taino ran to his aid.

Chapter 3:

ON THEIR WAY

The limo left the airport. Uncle Wilvo was gasping for air. "I'm sorry I took you away from your work in Philadelphia, but I've brought you back to Jamaica for a crucial reason," Uncle Wilvo said.

"I know, Uncle Wilvo. I will do my best to talk about Dad and his books at the book fair," T. L. said.

"Dat's not why I've begged you to come," Uncle Wilvo said.

"No?" T. L. said.

"Have you ever heard of Jamaican obeah?" Uncle Wilvo asked.

"Isn't that a breakfast dish?" T. L. kidded.

"It's witchcraft! Jamaican witchcraft!" Uncle Wilvo exclaimed.

"Of course. Yes, sir!"

Uncle Wilvo informed him, "In tree days, a witch in Kata Cove intends to unleash a duppy ghost pirate army and apocalypse upon di land! She is bringing dem back from di dead to help her find a sword known as di Iron Thorn."

"A duppy ghost pirate army? Really, Uncle Wilvo?" T. L. chuckled.

Uncle Wilvo continued, "Not just any duppies, Terry! She will raise an army from di ferocious pirates dat died during di Battle at Kata Cove! Di battle took place in di year 1655. Di only person who can stop dis nightmare from happening is you!"

"Me? Why?" T. L. asked.

Uncle Wilvo responded, "Because you are di direct descendant of Kata di Warrior King! And only you have di power to command his magic sword, di Iron Thorn! Di witch has the help of a wizard, a gangster, and a large pig."

"This is a joke, right?" T. L. laughed.

"No joke, Terry! All real! All true! And pray dat she does not command di cauldron to bring forth *di ting!*" Uncle Wilvo exclaimed.

"What 'ting' are you talking about, Uncle Wilvo?" T. L. asked.

Uncle Wilvo grabbed T. L. by his wrist. "Di Evil Ting, an unspeakable horror, Terry Lee!" Uncle Wilvo whimpered.

Taino looked out of his driver's side window and was shocked to see a ghoulish-looking person dressed like a pirate and a large pig running in the woods. Taino turned to T. L. and Uncle Wilvo, frightened. "I don't like no obeah and witchcraft talkin' round mi! You gwan talk obeah, you can drive dis limousine yaself! I will walk!" Taino swore.

"OK, Taino! Mi sorry; I will shut up! Keep drivin'! Keep drivin', please!" Uncle Wilvo reassured Taino.

Uncle Wilvo gave T. L. Dr. Barrett's old bamboo briefcase. T. L. looked in the briefcase and saw a folder that read, "DR. BARRETT'S LAND PAPERS." He also saw a children's book titled *Kata the Warrior King*, an old tape recorder, and an old framed photo. Uncle Wilvo whispered, "Dese are now yours. Der is a lot for you to learn. Read and listen to dese materials as soon as you can." T. L. looked at the old photo of five youthful-looking people: four men and one woman.

"Dese are an extraordinary group of people. Dey are di Iron Thorn Defenders. We protect Kata's magic sword. Your father kept di legend of Kata a secret from you in fear of di deadly legacy. Dis, of course, is mi and your father. Dis is Dr. Liang, Dr. Venables, and dis, dis is Lady Crawlene Sands. She's turned obeah witch, and she is back!" Uncle Wilvo fumed. They were all holding up their fists, showing off impressive gold Kata Magic Rings.

Uncle Wilvo took his Kata Magic Ring off his finger, put it on T. L.'s finger, and tightly held his hand. "Dis ring is one of Kata's magic rings! It is your birthright, and dere are nine more dat you must acquire! Dis one can help you learn di tings you need to know quicker. When you review dese materials, turn di ring on your finger counterclockwise two times. However, if you can't take what di ring is helping teach you, turn it clockwise twice," Uncle Wilvo disclosed.

Uncle Wilvo held up the land papers folder. "Den meet me tomorrow afternoon at di Barrett House on your father's land. Tell Taino to take you dere! Understand?" Uncle Wilvo said.

"Yes, sir!" T. L. replied.

Chapter 4:

KATA COVE

The limo drove through a stretch of dense fog. The fog suddenly cleared, and the limo pulled up to a fork in the road. On the left side was a large sign that read: To BUCCANEER & PIRATE PIER; there was a skull and crossbones flag on the sign. On the right side of the road, another sign read: To KATA COVE. The limo made a right turn.

The limo arrived at the breathtaking Kata Cove seaside mansion of husband-and-wife hosts Gerald and Leelah Sharp. The classy-looking couple, both in their sixties, were the owners of the Sharp Jamaican Coffee Company. The crowded Kata Cove Book Fair was underway on their spacious front lawn. A children's choir was finishing the Jamaican national anthem: "Jamaica, Jamaica, Jamaica, land we love!"

T. L. was ushered to the front of the crowd, where there was a stage flanked by tables with authors seated. T. L. recognized two distinguished gentlemen, Dr. Liang and Dr. Venables, from the picture. They were sitting on the stage, and they nodded to him. Dr. Liang and Dr. Venables, both medical doctors in their seventies, were wearing Kata Magic Rings as they wiped away tears.

"It's young Barrett; he's here," Dr. Liang said in an Asian accent.

"His education begins. I don't envy him. Let's chant one more time," Dr. Venables said in his British accent.

Dr. Liang and Dr. Venables said in unison, "We are the Iron Thorn Defenders. No harm will come to Kata's sword! Sworn to the Thorn! Woyo!" They performed a Kata hand salute.

Mr. Sharp walked on the stage and to the microphone. "Our last guest of honor has arrived! Kata Cove is proud to present the son of a great Jamaican, the late Reverend Dr. Leonard E. Barrett Sr. In Philadelphia, Pennsylvania, dey call him 'di Jamerican in Charge.' We welcome him back to him hometown. From Philly, Mr. Terry Lee Barrett is here. A few words, please, Mr. Barrett!" Mr. Sharp said.

The crowd applauded loudly! T. L. walked up to the microphone. "Thank you. I am proud to return to the most beautiful place in the world: Kata Cove, Jamaica! You may know that Philadelphia, Pennsylvania, has been my father's and my home for years, but only in body. My father's spirit will always be here in Kata Cove, as well as my own! I realized I hadn't been back here since I was a baby. Before I was 'Yankee raised' in Philly!" The crowd laughed.

Someone in the crowd yelled out, "Di Kata has returned! Hail to di Kata!" The crowd gleefully responded with lively forward-pointing thumbs-up signs. "Hail to di Kata! Hail—"

"Hey, all right, everyone quiet down!" Mr. Sharp interrupted.

"Aww! Booo!" The crowd moaned in disappointment.

"I'm sorry, Mr. Barrett. Seems to be a jokester in the crowd. A big round of applause for Terry Lee!" Mr. Sharp said. The crowd roared with cheers and applause for T. L., which frightened him.

T. L. was led to a table with his father's books stacked on it. People lined up with their own Dr. Barrett books, and T. L. started signing them. At the microphone, Mr. Sharp continued, "Now, ladies and gentlemen, my daughter Imani Sharp has something to say from her Save the Caribbean booth across the lawn."

Imani Sharp, the beautiful and brilliant daughter of Gerald and Leelah Sharp, was standing in the Save the Caribbean booth with a microphone in hand. She was flanked by four uniformed maritime friends from out of town: Captain Phoebe Olivia Penn, Maria Dolphi, Barbara Wilson, and Sidney James. They all had clipboards in their hands to help sign up supporters.

"Hi, everyone! As we all know, across the Caribbean, we have experienced stronger hurricanes and higher temperatures! We are in a climate crisis, and the Caribbean is one of the most vulnerable regions! Please stop by our STC booth and support. We are handing out complimentary bottles of hand sanitizer today as well! Thank you!" Imani declared in her sweet Jamaican accent.

T. L.'s attention was swept away by the sight of Imani. As she talked, she seemed to be moving in slow motion in his lovestruck eyes. The Caribbean breeze slowly blew her hair around her beautiful brown honey-colored face. She was statuesque in her sleeveless floral-printed dress and stood like a Jamaican goddess. T. L. felt that he knew Imani from somewhere and tried to recall exactly where.

T. L.'s stunned attention was broken when he saw a shift in the crowd in front of him and a strange figure walking in his direction. Children were following and laughing as the man strutted. It was Morgan Gritch, a menacing-looking British-born master magician, a wizard in training, and concert promoter who worked for the Jamaican gangster Layton Lafontant. He also referred to himself as "Captain" for publicity's sake. Gritch was dressed in a dazzling black seventeenth-century pirate outfit with swords in his belt. He was tall and stocky with shoulder-length bleached-blond hair. His skin seemed slightly discolored, as he was wearing what appeared to be a cheap spray-on tan. Two women in pirate costumes walked with Gritch, handing out flyers. One of the women did an acrobatic flip and accidentally knocked Gritch's pirate hat off his head, revealing thinning hair combed over a to hide a big bald spot.

Gritch sang a sea shanty, "I was told we cruise the seas for Jamaican gold. We'd fire no guns, shed no tears. Now I'm a broken man on a Kata Cove pier. The last of Barrett's privateers!"

The annoying Gritch walked behind T. L., interrupting him. "Hello, Barrett the privateer!" Gritch said in his bold, hard British drawl.

"Who are you supposed to be, a cheap Henry Morgan the pirate impersonator or something? Aren't you hot in that getup?" T. L. said.

"I like it hot, Privateer. Don't ye? The name's Gritch…Captain Morgan Gritch," Gritch growled.

"Captain Grinch? Captain Morgan Grinch!" T. L. chuckled.

"Oh, that's a good joke, Barrett. I've never heard that one before," Gritch stated.

"I noticed that you have two plastic swords in your belt. Seadog props?" T. L. laughed.

Gritch bent over T. L.'s shoulder. "What do ye know about swords?" Gritch said.

T. L. held his nose. "Yo, man, your breath! That must be authentic too. I know the difference between real swords and toy swords. I was a college champ in fencing at Temple University in Philly."

"I'm impressed, Barrett, but you wouldn't expect me to bring real swords to these proceedings. However, these will do for a match. Why don't we give these folks a demonstration?" Gritch said.

"No, that would not be appropriate at this time, and I know you're in no hurry to be bested. You make a great clown," T. L. said. He handed Gritch money.

Gritch glared at T. L, who retracted the money. "So Dr. Barrett's your father?" Gritch said.

"My late father, OK?" T. L. said, annoyed by the incredibly rude Gritch.

"My condolences." Gritch yawned.

T. L. felt sick and looked at the port-a-potty area, where there were long lines. He got up from his chair. "Folks, nature calls; I'll be back," T. L. said.

Gritch clamped down on T. L.'s shoulder and showed him a flyer in his other hand. "Wait. Please come to this affair. Ye know, the First Annual Buccaneer and Pirate Festival starts in three days at Buccaneer and Pirate Pier right down the road. We have the Bucca Jam Party tomorrow night, and you are our special guest," Gritch demanded.

T. L. removed Gritch's hand from his shoulder and snatched the flyer. "I'll make an individual effort. OK, aye, aye, Captain," T. L. said sarcastically.

"Aye, aye, privateer! Now walk, don't run! You might hurt yourself!" Gritch badgered him.

T. L. walked toward the property wall. He noticed a flashy-dressed man wearing large purple sunglasses walk up to Imani. It was Layton Lafontant, a Jamaican gangster whom she did not like, and she immediately walked away from him. She left her booth and stood beside Taino, who had a *Kata the Warrior King* book in his hand. She saw T. L. walking up, and she grabbed the book out of Taino's hand. "I'll get you another one," Imani said. T. L. walked toward the property fence, passing between Imani and a booth selling Kata and Empress Iyadola crown replicas. Imani showed T. L. the book. "I need dis book signed?" Imani said.

"I can do that," T. L. replied. T. L. looks into Imani's eyes, and she into his. "How do spell your name?" T. L. asked.

"Oh, I'm sorry. I-M-A-N-I. Make it out to 'Imani and the kids,' " Imani said.

" 'Imani and the kids,' OK. The kids' names are?" T. L. said.

"Oh, there are too many for you to write," Imani said.

"Oh?" T. L. said. T. L. handed her the signed book.

Imani poked T. L. with the pen. "Thank you, Kata!" Imani said.

"Excuse me?" T. L. said.

"I said thank you, Kata," Imani said. Imani took a Kata crown off the replica table and placed it on T. L.'s head. "Fit for a king!" Imani said.

"Kata, Kata, Kata," T. L. said.

"Guess you've heard a lot of dat lately. I would be honored if you could visit the Kata Cove School tomorrow. The kids are putting on a play in your honor," Imani said.

Taino interrupted and handed T. L. his Terry Love DJ promotion flyer from Philly. "Dis fell out of your backpack, mon. What a name, Terry Love!" Taino smirked.

"I've changed that to just DJ T. L. The Terry Love thing is a bit dated," T. L. said. He put the flyer in his shirt pocket. "Tomorrow it is, Imani. Listen, Imani and Taino, I'm not feeling too good. Please excuse me," T. L. said. He trotted behind the property wall and bent over, throwing up.

A police car with emergency lights flashing pulled up to the front of the Sharp Mansion. Captain Frank Ridge, a tough-looking policeman, got out, followed by other police. Captain Ridge headed to the stage. T. L. peered around the property wall and watched Captain Ridge take the mic. "As you all are probably aware, about sixteen tons of very expensive Sharp Jamaican Coffee beans have been stolen from a barge off the coast of Kata Cove! I want you all to know that we will find these thieves and pirates! 'Bad man haffi run!' " The crowd joined Captain Ridge's well-known Kata Cove chant: "Dey cyan't have no fun!"

Someone in the crowd yelled, "Di Kata is here! Di Kata will catch dem!"

Captain Ridge looked for the yeller. "Now don't start dat! We don't want to scare off our guest of honor!" Captain Ridge and the crowd laughed, and they all turned and stared at T. L., who ducked back behind the property wall, freaked out.

Chapter 5:

LADY CRAWLENE SANDS, OBEAH WITCH

T. L. backed away from the property wall. He was stopped in his tracks by Lady Crawlene Sands, the obeah witch. She was wearing a long black dress and a colorful head wrap with two parrots named Ackee and Salt on her shoulders. T. L. was taken aback by her sudden appearance. "Young Barrett, cyan ya sign dis book?" Lady Crawlene said. She handed T. L. a tattered *Kata the Warrior King* book. "Sign di book, please. Write it ta Lady Crawlene Sands, dat's mi, an' here are some cookies," Lady Crawlene said. Crawlene presented T. L. a small bag of foul-smelling cookies.

"Oh, no, thanks. I don't…" T. L. said.

Crawlene put a cookie in T. L.'s mouth. Though smelly and freaky in appearance, T. L. found them delicious. "Wow, where did you get these cookies?" T. L. asked.

Lady Crawlene grabbed the "DJ Terry Love" promotion flyer out of his shirt pocket. "Dis is a nice picture of you on dis flyer. Tyank you for givin' it to mi. Please sign ya name on dis flyer first," Lady Crawlene hissed.

Crawlene handed T. L. an old quill pen and inkwell. T. L. almost dropped the inkwell, and the black ink got all over his hands. He put the inkwell on a tree stump and attempted to sign the book but applied too much pressure and broke the pen.

"Oops, I'm sorry. I broke your pen," T. L. said. T. L. looked for Crawlene, but she was no longer there.

"Here I am, young mon!" Lady Crawlene said.

T. L. peered through the woods and saw Crawlene standing forty feet from him. "Lady Crawlene? Here's your book!" T. L. said. As he entered the woods, he heard the snort of a pig nearby.

Crawlene was suddenly a hundred yards away. "Hurry, bwoy! Hurry!" Lady Crawlene said.

When T. L. turned to leave the woods, Crawlene was suddenly right in front of him. "Did ya sign it?" Lady Crawlene asked.

"No, the pen broke," T. L. said.

"Did ya eat di cookie?" Lady Crawlene asked.

"Yes. Thank you. These are delicious, the best smelly cookies. Can you come back to the fair?" T. L. said.

"Come back? Yu di one who come back! Mind yaself, young mon; ya said ya would sign di book! So ya no sign it? Ya lie! Lie gwan catch ya!" Lady Crawlene scolded.

A large pig named Monty trotted up next to Crawlene. Tied around the pig's neck was a Kata Magic Ring. "Wha' ya scared ah, Monty di pig?" Lady Crawlene said.

T. L. had had enough, and he turned to leave, but Lady Crawlene clicked her fingers. "Eyes closed!" Lady Crawlene said. T. L.'s eyes closed. "Do ya see di Cauldron of Gold?" Lady Crawlene asked.

"The what?" T. L. asked.

In a dream state, T. L. was underwater, floating through shipwrecks. He saw something huge, gold, and bright in front of him, but he couldn't make out what it was. T. L. opened his eyes in a sweat. "OK, I'm getting out of here!" T. L. said.

"Don't move!" Lady Crawlene said.

T. L. found it challenging to move. Crawlene pulled out a machete and threw it at T. L., and he caught it, to his surprise. "Back up against di tree der!" Lady Crawlene demanded. Monty, the pig, snorted loudly, intimidating T. L.

"OK, I'm backing up against the tree!" T. L. said. Crawlene pulled out a knife and threw it at T. L. The Kata Magic Ring on T. L.'s finger forced his hand to react in self-defense, deflecting the knife into a tree with the machete. T. L. looked at the Kata Magic Ring on his hand in shock. "What the—" T. L. said.

"Could it be? Young mon, wield di machete tree times!" Lady Crawlene said. T. L. wielded the machete in a circular motion and accidentally hit a branch; the branch fell to the ground, propelling a rock up a tree, which struck a parrot, which took flight and landed on a mango. The mango dropped on the pig's head, pissing it off.

"Yes…yes…Kata! Kata! Now, listen, mi gwan ta protect ya from wicked an' evil forces. In exchange fa mi protection, ya will deliva to mi di Iron Thorn an di Cauldron of Gold. Dey will be better under mi protection for safe keepins. Now, a duppy ghost gwan follah ya for a while! A duppy ghost, a livin' ghost, ya understand? Gwan follah ya! See?" Lady Crawlene said.

Lady Crawlene pointed to her left into the shadows, and a male duppy ghost was standing there. It was a big, muscular duppy ghost with wild hair, swirling yellow eyes, sharp teeth, and an eerie orange glow. He was wearing tattered seventeenth-century pirate garb.

"Him name is Kriplin, di duppy ghost pirate!" Lady Crawlene hissed.

"Kriplin? What? A duppy ghost pirate, ma'am? That's entirely un- necessary!" T. L. said.

"Ya laugh, but Kriplin di duppy ghost pirate gwan follah yah! Mi put a spell on ya! Di only way ya could break mi spell is if ya had a Kata Magic Ring 'pon ya fingah. Ah ring like di one aroun' Monty di pig's neck," Lady Crawlene said.

"You mean a ring like this?" T. L. said. T. L. held up the Kata ring on his finger.

Lady Crawlene looked shocked, and Monty began squealing loudly at T. L. "Lady Crawlene, could you get a grip on that pig?" T. L. asked. T.

L. looked for Crawlene, but she had disappeared. However, Monty and Kriplin were still there. "Hey, piggly wiggly," T. L. said.

"Snort!" Pig Monty said.

"This little piggy went to the market, and this little piggy stayed home?" T. L. said. "Snort! Snort!" Pig Monty said.

"This little piggy had…jerk pork?" T. L. said. T. L. ran for it, with Monty and Kriplin chasing him in wild abandon. He saw an opening out of the woods. T. L. jumped and fell onto the road, sliding into the legs of one of the policemen stationed in front of the Sharp Mansion.

"Are you all right?" the policeman asked.

"Yes, I'm fine! Just fine, Officers!" T. L. said. He got up with the machete and then noticed that the Kata ring that was on Monty the pig's neck was now at his feet. He picked up the ring and walked past the police.

Chapter 6:

THE MAKING OF THE IRON THORN

In his Wells Mansion guest bedroom, T. L. opened the bamboo briefcase and took out the *Kata the Warrior King* children's book. T. L. read to himself out loud, "Kata is our Jamaican warrior, who fought terrible pirates and duppies. He became the king and protector of Kata Cove. He courted then wedded Empress Iyadola. Empress Iyadola was known as the Caller of Nature because she could call wild animals to her aid with her cow horn known as the Magic Golden Abeng. Kata created a magic sword known as the Mighty Iron Thorn. The Iron Thorn would obey Kata when he said the magic words, 'nyaka-nyaka!' The Iron Thorn could fight on its own when Kata commanded!"

T. L. turned to the page entitled "Kata's and Empress Iyadola's Magic Tings." The page showed labeled drawings of the Iron Thorn; Kata's ten magic rings; the Cauldron of Gold; Empress Iyadola's magic necklace, wristband, and Magic Golden Abeng; a pile of Ashanti gold; and the Brace of Powers. "This Kata should have opened a jewelry store in Philly," T. L. said.

He turned the page to see a drawing entitled *Kata and Empress Iyadola in Love*. It showed a picture of Kata and his wife, Empress Iyadola, embracing. T. L. looked at the last page. It was a picture of Kata standing, pointing, and stating, "Ya gwan learn to respeck di Kata, mon!" There was a water well in the background.

T. L. took out the cassette recorder. He took a cassette tape with the words PLEASE LISTEN written on it. He put the cassette in and pressed play. He heard his father's voice on the cassette. "Son, this is your father. If you are playing this tape, it means that I am no longer present, and your uncle Wilvo has summoned you to Kata Cove in an emergency. Son, I am sorry that I never told you about Kata, but please understand it was for a good reason—a reason that you will have to learn about now. The Kata ring that Uncle Wilvo gave you will help you visualize the story I am about to tell you. Turn the ring counterclockwise twice," Dr. Barrett said in his beautiful Jamaican accent.

T. L. turned the ring counterclockwise twice. In a dream state, T. L. saw a fleet of British ships on the sea.

"Our adventure begins in the year 1655, when a thirty-eight-ship fleet from England, led by Sir Admiral William Penn Sr. and General Robert Venables, sailed to the Caribbean from England with eight thousand soldiers and took the island of Jamaica from the Spanish Crown. The word *Jamaica* is originally a native Jamaican Taino word meaning 'the land of wood and water,' " Dr. Barrett said.

In his dream state, T. L. was in 1655 Jamaica. He was standing behind a crate on the Port Royal Pier. Pirates walked by him.

Dr. Barrett continued, "At the time, Jamaica's Port Royal was the buccaneer and pirate capital of the world, home to ruthless cutthroats and scalawags."

T. L. was now transported to a Jamaican warrior community at Kata Cove. The warriors and their families were playing with children, cooking food, and practicing fighting. Dr. Barrett continued, "Jamaica was also the home of a tough group of Jamaican warriors who would not remain enslaved. They ran off and lived in the Blue Mountains with the native Taino people. One of their mightiest warriors was known as Kata. The word *kata* is an old Jamaican word that means 'king' or 'protector'!"

T. L. now saw a montage of Kata's heroics as Dr. Barrett continued. "Kata was a ferocious pirate and duppy ghost fighter. He had the strength of a lion and the speed of an Olympian. He defeated plundering pirates and slew demonic duppies. Among the many duppies he slew were the Kingston Ghouls and the Ten-Eyed Maggoty Bull. However, as more pirates arrived and more duppies challenged, Kata needed more power!"

T. L. was watching Kata from behind a barrel in Kata's 1655 sword-making shed. T. L. saw a crowd from the community looking into Kata's shed, watching him make the Iron Thorn, as Dr. Barrett continued. "The Mighty Iron Thorn lethal-magic sword was created to assist Kata in battle!"

T. L. heard a booming voice: "Kata, prepare for a visit from Nan, di Queen Enchantress!" Nan, di Queen Enchantress, a regal-looking sorceress, entered the shed with a large burlap sack and stood next to Kata. She reached into the sack and produced a giant dead vulture. She whispered into Kata's ear and handed him the vulture. Dr. Barrett continued, "With a special visit from the island's fiercest warrior and obeah queen, Nan, di Queen Enchantress, Kata created the Iron Thorn. The Iron Thorn was forged with the carcass of a huge Jamaican vulture, also known as the mighty John Crow, blood from Kata's hand, mysterious iron ore, and ancient sorcery, and it is said to have been hit by lightning during its creation. The deadly sword could fight by itself on Kata's command."

The Iron Thorn was placed on a table, and Kata stepped back. Kata commanded it, "*Iron Thorn, mi command you to mi hand!*" The Iron Thorn leaped from the table into Kata's hand. Kata commanded it again: "*Iron Thorn, mi command you to nyaka-nyaka!*"

The sword leaped out of Kata's hand, flew through the air, and plowed through the shed wall. The Iron Thorn missed warriors who were standing outside. The Iron Thorn flew by Kata's astonished warriors and up into the sky. Kata calmly walked out and watched the Iron Thorn cut off the tops of trees in its path. In the distance, he heard a bird squawk, apparently hit by the sword. The now-bloody Iron Thorn turned in the air and headed straight back to Kata at high speed. Right before it appeared that the bloody Iron Thorn would hit Kata, he raised his hand. Kata commanded it, "*Iron*

Thorn, mi command you to cease and sekkle!" The Iron Thorn stopped in midair right in front of Kata's heart.

Kata commanded it again: "*Iron Thorn, mi command you to mi hand!*" The Iron Thorn leaped back into Kata's hand, and he raised it in the air as the warrior community cheered, but his wife, Empress Iyadola, looked on, shocked and concerned.

T. L. was now on a pirate ship hiding behind a stack of ropes. Pirates were standing in a circle around a map of Kata Cove. "The Iron Thorn was the envy of unscrupulous pirates. In an attempt to steal the Iron Thorn, a surprise attack was planned," Dr. Barrett said.

T. L. was now behind a boulder on a hill overlooking Kata's wedding anniversary ceremony. The ceremony was attended by hundreds, including a long procession of dancers and drummers.

Dr. Barrett continued, "The Battle at Kata Cove was launched during Kata's flamboyant wedding anniversary ceremony." T. L. saw Kata and Empress Iyadola holding up their baby at an altar as the crowd cheered. "Anticipating an afternoon of celebration, Kata locked the Iron Thorn away that fateful day. Suddenly, pirate ships appeared from behind the cliffs. Pirates also appeared from the wooded areas and attacked. The attack surprised Kata. A Caribe man with a blowgun darted Kata with a sedative. A pirate appeared from behind Kata and hit him in the head with a blunt instrument, and Kata was knocked unconscious!"

T. L. was now on a pirate ship hiding behind a stack of ropes. Pirates walked by with the captured Empress Iyadola in chains. "During the bloody battle, the pirates captured Kata's beloved wife, Empress Iyadola, and took her to their ships stationed at sea," Dr. Barrett said.

T. L. looked out to sea. Behind the pirate ship, T. L. saw the Cauldron of Gold tethered to a fortified barge. "The pirates also stole Kata's anniversary present, the fabled Cauldron of Gold, the combined gift of the Jamaican warrior leaders. The giant, ten-foot, solid-gold cauldron had mystical powers!" Dr. Barrett said.

T. L. in his dream state saw a shadowy figure standing inside his bedroom. Frightened, he turned his Kata ring twice clockwise. T. L. woke up, turned on a flashlight, and saw the shadowy figure wearing Kata's African crown and kente-cloth vest. "Kata?" T. L. asked.

There was a loud knock on the bedroom door, and T. L. turned the flashlight toward the door. When he turned the flashlight back to the shadowy figure, it was gone. A large window was suddenly wide open, and the broad bedroom curtains billowed in the warm evening breeze. T. L. closed the window. He put everything back into the bamboo briefcase and closed it. "Who is it?" T. L. said.

"It's Dr. Liang!" Dr. Liang said. Dr. Liang opened the door, turned on the light, rushed into the room, and pulled up a chair next to T. L. "Hello, Terry Lee. I'm Dr. Liang!" Dr. Liang said.

"Hello, Dr. Liang," T. L. said.

"I hope I'm not disturbing you," Dr. Liang said.

"Um?" T. L. said, feeling completely disturbed.

"I was a longtime friend of your father. I was at your father's funeral in Philadelphia," Dr. Liang said.

T. L. shook Dr. Liang's hand. Dr. Liang was astonished to see two Kata rings on T. L.'s fingers. T. L. noticed a Kata ring on Dr. Liang's finger. "Thanks for coming to my father's funeral," T. L. said.

"They were a great credit to the human race, your mother and father. The fact that they lived long, healthy, and productive lives is a beautiful thing. Beautiful indeed," Dr. Liang said.

"I think they were too good for this crazy world," T. L. said.

"A crazy world, for sure. However, their spirits are at rest now! They join your ancestors and will continue to be a powerful force in your life! Our lives! We stand on the shoulders of giants! Your dad was a man of peace," Dr. Liang said.

"Yes, he always spoke out against war. His favorite saying was, 'Put your sword back in its place, for all who draw the sword will die by the sword.' He was also concerned about what greed does to people!" T. L. said.

T. L. and Dr. Liang said, "Greed is a bottomless pit that exhausts the person in an endless effort to satisfy the need without ever reaching satisfaction." They both laughed.

"This is my favorite: 'Give evil nothing to oppose, and it will disappear by itself.' That's from the Chinese Tao philosophy," Dr. Liang said.

"Wow, that's a good one. Never heard that one before," T. L. said.

"So you know why you're here then?" Dr. Liang asked.

"I'm beginning to get the picture. I now know why my father did not tell me about the Kata legend until today," T. L. said.

"Today?"

"Look, Dr. Liang, I am a deejay. I live in Philadelphia, sir. It's time for me to get paid, not slayed! I am getting out of here first thing in the morning! I'm sorry—" T. L. said.

Interrupting, Mrs. Sharp knocked on the bedroom door. "Hello, honored guests! We would like to have you for dinner."

T. L. hugged Mrs. Sharp. "Thank you so much, Mrs. Sharp!" T. L. said. T. L. rushed out of the room. Mrs. Sharp looked on, bewildered.

Chapter 7:

DI MOOF-KA-ZOOT

Meanwhile, in the woods at Lady Crawlene's lair, Lady Crawlene was preparing dinner. Lady Crawlene was wearing an apron and cooking Caribbean cuisine on a woodburning stove. Three duppies were seated at a table watching Lady Crawlene cook and looking very hungry. Her lair was packed with books, flickering candles, spooky trinkets, and old bamboo furniture.

Outside her lair about one hundred yards away was Morgan Gritch hiding behind a tree. Gritch was equipped with a futuristic-looking Hausbell listening device that looked like a space gun, and he was pointing it toward Lady Crawlene's lair window. He was wearing headphones and looking through binoculars, listening in on Lady Crawlene's creepy dinner party.

Outside, Gritch saw Kriplin walking down the path and into Crawlene's lair. "Sorry I'm late," Kriplin said.

Lady Crawlene pulled Kriplin aside. "What did ya find out, Kriplin?" Lady Crawlene asked.

"I went to Gritch's secret place, and he didn't see me," Kriplin said. "Gritch has gone nutters; either he was talking to himself or to someone that I could not see. He said he wants to take his magic act to another level. He's studying how to become a wizard online. What does he mean, *online*?"

"Never mind dat. Go on—what else him say?" Lady Crawlene snapped.

"He said he had channeled the spirits of alchemist wizards from the Invisible College of the Royal Society of London that existed in the 1660s," Kriplin said.

"Have mercy!" Lady Crawlene agonized.

"He said he's been reading about transforming gold, if he can find some, into a potion that, when ingested, will give him unstoppable superpowers!" Kriplin said.

"What, he knows about di ancient African alchemy process known as di Moof-Ka-Zoot? He would need rare Ashanti gold and di Cauldron of Gold to perform dat ritual, and only Barrett knows where the Ashanti gold and di cauldron is hidden!" Lady Crawlene said.

"Ashanti, Moof-Ka what? I do not understand," Kriplin said.

"Oh, shut up, Kriplin, ya ruin di dinna!" Lady Crawlene screamed.

Outside, Kriplin wrote the words *Ashanti gold and the Cauldron of Gold* on a notepad.

Chapter 8:

BAD GUYS
ON THE BEACH

The next morning presented a beautiful Caribbean day with a brilliant blue sky and a warm breeze. Taino was washing the limo in the driveway. T. L. walked up to him with a cup of Sharp coffee in hand. "Good morning, Sir Taino," T. L. said.

"Di mon Barrett, ah good mornin', sir!" Taino said.

"Man, this is the best coffee!" T. L. said.

"Yes, Sharp Jamaican Coffee is di best! Di Sharp family coffee plant is right up di road. Ya, mon, dem internationally known!" Taino said.

"You know how much it costs for a pound of Sharp Jamaican Coffee in at Old City Coffee, in Philly? Obscene prices! Yesterday, Captain Ridge said that someone stole sixteen tons of Sharp Jamaican Coffee off a barge at Kata Cove. Taino, I did the math; that's like two million US dollars' worth of coffee they stole!" T. L. said.

"Dat's a ridiculous amount of money! Dem guys need to be caught, mon!" Taino asserted as he slammed his washrag on the limo hood.

"Boy, do I need this. I hardly slept last night," T. L. said.

"Wha' happen, food too spicy?" Taino joked.

"No, they started telling ghost stories; they got me spooked! Heard some sounds outside that kept me up all night. Duppies or something," T. L. said.

"Cha, mon. Mi nah like duppy stories. Especially at night, when duppies go boo!" Taino said. Taino's sudden arm extension knocked the coffee out of T. L.'s hand. "Oops, sorry bout dat, mon," Taino said.

T. L. wiped the coffee off his face and hands.

"I'm packing now and heading to the airport. Can you take me?" T. L. asked.

"You're leavin'?"

"I'm outta here. I've got to get back to Philly," T. L. said.

"What about Imani and di school kids? Mon, dey are expecting you today. You're di mon about here; people have been waitin' for your return. You cyan't up and leave dem," Taino said.

"Yeah, that Imani. Wow," T. L. said.

T. L. pulled out the Barrett land papers and showed them to Taino. "Taino, you know where Kata Cove Road is?" T. L. asked.

"Of course, yah, mon, mi know dat," Taino said.

"My father's land is there. I haven't been there since I was a kid. Can you take me there before we head to the airport?" T. L. asked.

"Of course, mon. I guess it's your land now. Come on, let's go."

Taino and T. L. got in the limo and drove off. T. L. pulled a swimming mask and snorkel out of his backpack. "What dat?" Taino said.

"A mask and snorkel. We have some time; I might as well go swimming at Kata Cove. It's on the water, right?" T. L. asked.

"Yes, but nobody swim dere," Taino said.

"Nobody swims there? Why not?" T. L. said.

"Dat water is cursed—a lot of mean fish dere. Sharks, barracudas, and big green crabs, ah bite you up good. It's an excellent place to fish but not to swim. Also, di water gets suddenly deep, a big steep drop-off. Sometime you see bones from where di fish eat men who try to swim dere," Taino said.

"What? Human bones? You're kidding!"

"Mi nah joke! Human bone, wash up 'pon di shore!" Taino said.

They drove through a wooded area and crossed over a river. They saw and heard a deejay's sound system playing the legendary Bob Marley song, "One Love."

"Oh, that's it!" T. L. said.

"Yah, mon, dat's di classic one! Roots, reggae nice, mon!" Taino said.

They drove out of the woods, and Kata Cove Beach, the Barrett House, and the Kata Cove School were in full view. It was breathtakingly beautiful. The Cove School was a wooden structure not far from the beach, and it was in session, loud and clear. T. L. looked at the old three-story wooden Barrett House on the hill behind the school. The house was bright lime green and appeared newly painted. "Taino, I remember being here many years ago. Wow, this is stunningly beautiful! Cursed, I don't think so!" T. L. said.

"Dis is where your land is! Your land starts here at the Kata wood tree, along di water, and it goes back pass di old Barrett House, a way back so," Taino said.

T. L. and Taino got out of the limo. Taino noticed a tough-looking young man named Face in swimming trunks pulling a rope out of the sea. At the water's edge, Face pulled in a fish trap. Face examined the trap; there were crabs in it. He also found an old pirate spyglass.

"You see dat guy? It's guys like dat going to screw us all!" Taino said.

"By fishing?" T. L. said.

"No, by stealin' fish, among other tings! Dat is your uncle Wilvo's fish trap! Him steal right out in di pure open!" Taino said. Taino jogged down to the beach and confronted Face. He grabbed him by the back of the neck and brought him up to T. L. Taino said to Face, "See dis mon here? Him father, Dr. Barrett, owns di land, and him back to claim it! And he will arrest anybody loitering and causing a disturbance! Ya understand?"

Face provocatively balanced the pirate spyglass on his middle finger, mocking T. L.

T. L. grabbed the pirate spyglass. "Hey, I don't want any problems, man. OK?"

"Ah, you di Yankee man, Barrett?" Face said.

"Watch how you address Mr. Barrett!" Taino said.

"What's your name?" T. L. asked.

"Mi name is Fyace!" Face said.

Taino let Face go. Face smirked and trotted to a waiting Jet Ski and rode out toward a yacht that was anchored out at sea. Taino got a text from Imani demanding to know where they were. He showed the text to T. L.

Unbeknownst to T. L., a sudden, thin light beam bolted out of one of his Kata Magic Rings, and it hit Face's Jet Ski. The Jet Ski exploded and catapulted Face forward in the air and onto the yacht. "What the..." T. L. said. T. L. didn't realize that his Kata Magic Ring had destroyed the Jet Ski. He noticed that one of the Kata rings had now turned a blood red. He tapped the ring, and it turned back to a gold color. T. L. took the old pirate spyglass, lifted it to his eye, and focused on the impressive yacht not far from shore. He tightened the focus on three people on the yacht. It was Layton Lafontant, Morgan Gritch, and Lady Crawlene Sands laughing at Face. They all had binoculars around their necks. They, too, didn't realize that the Kata Magic Ring had destroyed the Jet Ski.

On the deck of the yacht, they all look at the groggy Face in disbelief. "Bwoy, ya gwan have ta pay for dat Jet Ski outcha income! How it explode like dat? Ya naw take care of it, mon! OK, back ta business," Layton groused. They all looked at T. L. through their binoculars. "Look at Barrett! Him nah know what to tink! We are gwan scare him right back to Philly. So mi workin' on di exact location of di Cauldron of Gold. Mi now know it's really down der, and mi figured out a way ta bring it up! Den we can melt it down, and we will all be rich in gold!" Layton said.

"No, we won't melt down di cauldron! Dat's not di plan mi agree to! When we bring up di cauldron, mi will activate it and unleash mi duppy ghost pirate army! Dey will come out of di cauldron. Ya understand?" Lady Crawlene said.

"And I will perform the Moof-Ka-Zoot and bring forth di Evil Ting!" Gritch said.

"No, mi would neva do dat! Are ya crazy, Gritch? Di Evil Ting would kill us all! Why would we want ta do dat?" Lady Crawlene complained.

Gritch winked at Layton from behind Crawlene's back and twirled his fingers around his ears to signal that Crawlene was crazy. "Yes, we understand, Lady Crawlene! We will unleash di duppy ghost pirate army, and along wit di Iron Thorn, we will rule di world!" Layton said.

"Dat's right!" Lady Crawlene said.

Layton tossed Gritch a small tape recorder. "Time ta get ta work! Showtime, Gritchey!" Layton said. Gritch took out a phone and called T. L. and held the tape recorder speaker to the phone. T. L.'s phone rang, and he answered his phone on the beach.

"Hello?" T. L. said.

Gritch hit the play button on the tape recorder, and it was a recorded message with Uncle Wilvo's voice. "Hi, Terry Lee. Sorry mi missed you last night. Mi lost mi phone. I had to go to Kingston on business, but meet mi at di Bucca Jam Party tonight. It's essential, so you betta be der!" Gritch turned off the tape recorder.

"OK, Uncle Wilvo, I'll be there! Hello? Uncle Wilvo? He hung up, weird," T. L. said.

"Let's go. Imani is waiting," Taino said.

Chapter 9:

THE KATA COVE
SCHOOL

T. L. and Taino entered the class. The children were excited to see them as they performed in a play titled *Kata di Warrior King*. Children were standing and singing behind a large cardboard Cauldron of Gold. Two of the children were dressed up like Kata and Empress Iyadola.

The children sang,

> Kata was king of Kata Cove.
> He and Empress Iyadola were deeply in love.
> They lived during tragic times.
> Hard was their mountain to climb.
> Yah gwan learn to respeck mi!
> Hail to the Kata! Hail to Empress Iyadola!
> Forevah farward! Woyo!

The children screamed with excitement and give each other fist-and-thumb bumps. Imani, T. L., and Taino applauded. "Class, now politely, say hello to Taino and Terry!" Imani said.

"Hello, Taino and Terry!" the children said.

"And this is our exceptional guest, he is the son of the Reverend Doctor Leonard E. Barrett Sr., who wrote many books about Jamaica. Dr. Barrett wrote the book that we performed from today called *Kata the Warrior King*," Imani said.

"Hello, everyone. It is an honor to be here," T. L. said.

The kid that was dressed like Kata named Marcus gave T. L. the toy Iron Thorn. "Thank you!" T. L. said. T. L. raised the Iron Thorn in the air and then gave it back to Marcus.

Imani turned to Taino. "Take over. Play 'Now That We've Found Love' for them."

Taino played the piano as the kids sang along. Imani took T. L. by the hand and walked him outside. "That play was so cute!" T. L. said.

"Yes, in honor of Kata Week, we do this play every year. Glad you caught the end of it," Imani said.

"Sorry I was late," T. L. said.

"That was so sweet when Marcus and Louise gave you the Iron Thorn! It's all good when you help di children. Do you have any children?" Imani said.

"Haven't had time. It looks like you've got enough for both of us. Any of your own?" T. L. said.

"None of my own yet. These kids are like my kids for now," Imani said. Imani and T. L. looked at each other fondly.

"It's so beautiful here; this is unbelievable! I'm glad my father kept this place," T. L. said.

"Beautiful, yes, but the work is hard, Terry. As a visitor, things may look great. But there are real issues here: unemployment, medical care. Not the best future for some of the kids," Imani said.

T. L. looked at the Barrett House on the hill behind the school.

"That's your father's place. That's the house he grew up in and where you were born," Imani said.

"It's been a while. Come on, let's take a look," T. L. said.

"I don't know; your uncle Wilvo asked that no one goes around the house. He said he didn't want you to stay here during your visit because you would bring too much attention to it," Imani said.

"Imani, according to these documents, I own the place now," T. L. said, showing Imani the documents and deed.

They walked past the iron gate, and T. L. could see a well at the back of the property. He realized that it looked like the well on the last page of the *Kata the Warrior King* book. The house was well kept. T. L. tried the door: it was locked. He looked through the shaded window that had a KEEP OUT sign on it and saw and heard the back of the shadowy figure he had seen last night, whistling, cooking, and wearing Kata's African crown and vest! T. L. banged on the window. "Hey, Kata!" T. L. said. T. L. stumbled, feeling faint.

The bag of Lady Crawlene's cookies fell out of T. L.'s backpack, and Imani picked them up. She smelled the cookies and squeezed her nose in disgust. "Terry, are you all right?" Imani asked.

T. L. looked in the window for Kata, but he was gone. "I don't know! I'm still feeling a little sick and having some bad dreams," T. L. said.

"These nasty-smelling cookies are not helping you!" Imani said. Imani put the cookies in T. L.'s backpack.

"Yeah, and I did get them from a witch," T. L. said.

"A what?" Imani said.

"Imani, Kata said the magic words *nyaka-nyaka*. What do the words *nyaka-nyaka* mean?" T. L. asked.

"Catching up on your Kata education? The words *nyaka-nyaka* in Jamaican speak mean when a person does a piece of work poorly, using a cutting instrument, it is said that they nyaka-nyaka the work. This means that they have done it badly or unevenly. Let's see, how could I say it like an American?" Imani lightly smacked T. L. on his cheek. "It means, he'd mess you up, dude! Ha, that's what Kata did to evil pirates and duppies with his Iron Thorn." Imani laughed.

T. L. put his hand on his cheek. "Oh, what a nice guy this Kata was," T. L. said.

"Your father never told you about Kata? That's unbelievable!" Imani said.

"No, never told me anything until I got here. So Kata had a magic sword, a beautiful wife, and he was a ghostbuster? The pirates wanted the sword and kidnapped his wife, and now he haunts the area? Something like that?" T. L. said.

"Well, something like that. It's a great love story, don't you think?" Imani said.

"A love story? More like one of the scariest Halloween-type ghost stories of all time, Jamaican style!" T. L. said.

There was a cloudburst, and T. L. and Imani squeezed together under the porch roof to avoid the rain. "Don't you remember, Terry? The first and only time you came back here for a visit is when you were eight years old," Imani said.

"I remember now, Imani. I remember my father and Uncle Wilvo driving me here. They were having fun talking about the past. I remember I couldn't see past my nose because the woods were so thick, more than they are now. I remember you and me playing around this house, having so much fun and laughing so hard. When my father and Uncle Wilvo were busy doing something, somewhere, you and I kissed. I remember, Imani, when I kissed you on this porch. My first kiss ever," T. L. said. T. L. pulled Imani close and they kissed passionately.

"No, Terry, you're missing the point! It's a great tragic love story, worse than *Romeo and Juliet*!" Imani said.

"Really? And that's a good thing?"

"For their wedding anniversary, Kata created a beautiful magic necklace and wristband that could make Empress Iyadola disappear if she were in grave danger. She could then reappear to safety. However, di pirates attacked before Kata could give her di necklace and wristband. Of course, Empress Iyadola knew that she was getting an anniversary present, and she grabbed dem and put dem on before being kidnapped.

"While kidnapped on di pirate ship and tied to di Cauldron of Gold, di necklace began to pulsate with light, and Empress Iyadola disappeared!

Empress Iyadola reappeared on di shore at Kata Cove and looked for Kata. But it was too late. Sick and weak from being hit by a poison dart, Kata and a few of his warriors had already gone out to the pirate ship with di Iron Thorn to save her. All they saw was Empress Iyadola's crown of red hibiscus flowers in di water and thought that the pirates had killed her.

"Kata was so heartbroken, he jumped into di sea in search of his love. A school of fish tried to save Kata, but he did not want to be saved. That's why our favorite dish around here is called Kata fish in honor of those fish who tried to save Kata.

"Empress Iyadola was a Taino of great power and rank and the best swimmer on the island; she dove into the sea searching for Kata. She saw the sunken pirate ships and the Cauldron of Gold, but no trace of Kata. Empress Iyadola forbade Kata Jr. from using the Iron Thorn because she never trusted it. Though devastated, she would live on and fight bravely in Kata's honor against plundering pirates and wicked duppies. After a courageous life, Empress Iyadola died from her most lethal wound, a broken heart. She's buried at the ever-flowering red hibiscus bush on the hill there.

"When Empress Iyadola passed away, Kata Jr. became very distressed and decided to resume using the Iron Thorn for its intended purpose."

Imani started tearing up, and T. L. hugged her. "Now that's tragic! And now I *really* have to get back to Philly," T. L. said.

"Don't be scared, Terry. That's the children's version. Who knows what really happened," Imani said.

"Yeah, and who knows if history wants to repeat itself," T. L. said.

Taino suddenly walked around the corner of the house, frightening Imani and T. L. Taino threw Imani a five-foot bamboo pole. Taino also had a pole in hand. Taino and Imani skillfully play-fought martial arts style with the bamboo poles. "Um, excuse me, guys! My father never had any swords around when I was growing up! I would have seen this Iron Thorn if it were around!" T. L. said.

Imani knocked Taino down with her pole.

"Dem say dat your father hid di Iron Thorn, den he left for Philadelphia. So now dat your father is no longer with us, you are his descendant and di new Kata!" Taino said.

"You guys are serious! You believe that this legend is true?" T. L. said.

"Yes. There were pirates in Jamaica once. That's a legend, and that's true, isn't it?" Imani said.

"Yes. So where is the Iron Thorn?" T. L. asked.

"It's hidden, of course, and you should not speak of it. Your uncle Wilvo knows. Ask him, but keep it quiet, Terry," Imani said.

"Wow, if I could get ahold of that magic sword!" T. L. pondered as he looked at the well on the property.

Taino and Imani stared at T. L. "What would you do with it?" Imani and Taino said.

T. L. and Imani were startled by three motorcycles pulling up with a teenage dreadlocked cyclist in the lead. "Hey, Terry Love! I got a surprise for you! Dis is my man, Dreadlock Berky!" Taino said.

"Dey said you'd be here! Here's di mota I got fa Mr. Barrett!" Dreadlock Berky said.

"Nice! Very nice!" T. L. said. T. L. turned to Imani. "Well, what are you doing later? I have to meet Uncle Wilvo at that party tonight at Buccaneer and Pirate Pier. Why don't you come with me?" T. L. said.

"What? Why would your uncle Wilvo meet you there? Those are bad people at Buccaneer and Pirate Pier, DJ T. L.! There's an old saying round here: 'Badman haffi run, cyan't have nah fun, or they will feel the scorn of the Iron Thorn!' That saying goes way back, Terry! Away back!" Imani said.

"Uncle Wilvo just called and told me to meet him there. I have to talk to him about this land and this Kata stuff. It's a bit overwhelming, too overwhelming," T. L. said.

"Terry, think about this. Your uncle Wilvo was very upset when those jerks at Buccaneer and Pirate Pier announced having an annual pirate festival on the same week we here in Kata Cove celebrate Kata's and Empress Iyadola's lives!" Imani said.

"OK, maybe I won't meet him there," T. L. said.

Imani wrote her phone number down on a piece of paper. "Be careful at dat party, Terry. Call me early tomorrow if you can. It's great to see you again. Adieu, sweet Kata!" Imani said as she kissed him on his cheek.

Chapter 10:

PHOEBE OLIVIA PENN

T. L., Dreadlock Berky, and his friends raced down the parish coastline. T. L., in the lead, turned a sharp corner and came upon a sudden roadblock. T. L. spun out and fell off the bike but got right back up. The sign on the roadblock fence said ROAD CLOSED—SHARP JAMAICAN COFFEE LOADING ZONE AHEAD.

"Sorry about dat, Terry; they must have just put up dat roadblock—it wasn't dere before today," Dreadlock Berky said.

"Well, that was close," T. L. said.

"Let's take a break here before we head back," Dreadlock Berky said.

"Man, I'm dying to do some snorkeling," T. L. said.

T. L. took out his pirate spyglass and looked out to sea. Not far out to sea was an impressive seventy-foot research ship. Written on the side were the words *Explorer Penn Oceanography*, Philadelphia, Pennsylvania. "What the...that ship is from Philly! This is a coincidence that needs to be investigated. Dreadlock Berky, I hear there're sharks and barracudas in the water, and it's cursed. True?" T. L. asked.

"Cursed? Shark and barracuda? Not round here?" Dreadlock Berky said.

"You sure? Taino said you can't go in the water because you can get eaten," T. L. said.

"Taino? Him scared of di wata, mon! All ah we fish an' swim in di wata round here. Nottin' gwan eat yu. Gwan, mon, have fun!" Dreadlock Berky said.

T. L. spoke in his bad patois. "Dreadlock Berky, check mi bike, mon. Me take care ah you wit ah US money, cool?"

Dreadlock Berky and his friends laughed at T. L.'s attempt at speaking patois. "Yah, mon, mi cool here till ya get back. Just ah cool star," Dreadlock Berky said. T. L. trotted behind a palm tree and changed into his swim trunks and stuffed his street clothes into his backpack. He left his backpack with Dreadlock Berky.

T. L. swam out to the ship and climbed onto the ship's ladder. "Hello, hello, hello?" T. L. said. T. L. was startled by something in the water pulling at him. It was Captain Phoebe Olivia Penn, an oceanographer and descendant of the famous Penn family of England and Philadelphia.

Phoebe emerged wearing scuba gear. She was tall and athletic looking. She was followed by three associates: Maria Dolphi, a short, tough-talking student from South Philadelphia, and Barbara Wilson and Sidney James, both students from Jamaica.

"Sorry to frighten you. Can I help you?" Phoebe asked.

"Just looking for somebody from Philly!" T. L. said.

"There's two here from Philly! Hi, I'm Captain Phoebe Olivia Penn; I'm one of them. Allow me to formally introduce you to Doctors-to-Be Maria Dolfi, from South Philly, Barbara Wilson, from Montego Bay, and Sidney James, from Kingston, Jamaica," Phoebe said.

"My name is Terry, Terry Lee Barrett. They call me T. L. I live in Old City, Philly…right down the street from Independence Hall and the Liberty Bell," T. L. said.

Phoebe and Maria applauded and cheered. "We were at the book signing with Imani Sharp yesterday to get our books signed, but you ran off!" Phoebe said. Everyone laughed.

"Sorry, I was being hunted by pirates, witches, duppy ghosts, and a large pig. Wasn't feeling too good. However, I'm prepared to sign your books before I disembark!" T. L. said.

T. L. looked at a high-tech minisubmarine complete with a mechanical arm hanging on the side of the ship. "Somebody sure has brains in this family. You trying to catch the Jamaican Moby Dick?" T. L. asked.

"Nah, we are looking for some sunken items from cruise ships. Beer?" Phoebe said.

"Sure," T. L. said.

"Yo, Ska-Bot, a few brews, please!" Maria said. A Honda Asimo robot wearing a porkpie hat on its head came around the corner with ska music blasting from a speaker on its back. It bopped to the music before it opened a refrigerator and grabbed a tray of beers. It brought the beers to Maria. Ska-Bot disappeared around the corner.

"Waterproof?" T. L. laughed.

"So far. We only bring him out to show off to special guests!" Maria said.

"I want its autograph," T. L. said.

Around the corner, Ska-Bot looks across the deck and sees Kriplin trying to climb onto the ship. Kriplin is wearing a long-hooded raincoat. Ska-Bot quickly approaches Kriplin, shakes up a beer, pops the top, and sprays beer in Kriplin's face. Kriplin falls off the side of the ship and into the sea.

T. L. focused on two old pictures on the wall: a seventeenth-century ship captain and a man dressed in Quaker garb. "These men look familiar," T. L. said.

"They inspire and perspire us. It's Sir Admiral William Penn Sr.! You know, like in Pennsylvania. Sir Admiral William Penn Sr. and his troops took Jamaica from Spain in 1655," Phoebe said.

"Yes, and the other man is his son William Penn Jr. Sir Admiral William Penn Sr. didn't like his son because he became a Quaker, an antiwar peacenik. When Sir Admiral William Penn Sr. died, the king of England owed him a lot of money. So the king paid his son back with land, granting him land in America called Pennsylvania. William Penn Jr. was an early champion of democracy in Philadelphia, Pennsylvania," T. L. added.

Phoebe, Maria, Barbara, and Sidney applauded. "Dr. Barrett's son speaks! Profound knowledge, Terry! Couldn't have explained it better myself!" Phoebe said.

"So there'd be no Philadelphia and no Declaration of Independence without Jamaica!" Sidney said. Phoebe, Maria, and Barbara laughed hard at Sidney's revelation.

T. L.'s concentration drifted away as he had accidentally turned his Kata magic ring counterclockwise twice. He continued to look at William Penn Jr.'s picture and heard him speak, but Phoebe, Maria, Barbara, and Sidney didn't hear him.

"The Quakers also promoted the phrase 'Speak truth to power,' which means speaking out to those in authority when they try to trample on your rights. Forty years after my death, the Quakers organized and fought against slavery with the belief that love can overcome hatred," William Penn Jr.'s ghost said.

T. L. inadvertently turned his Kata magic ring clockwise twice. He turned to Phoebe. "Yeah, I couldn't have said that better myself. Cool phrase—speak truth to power!" T. L. said.

"What?" Phoebe said.

"Didn't you say that?" T. L. asked.

"Huh?" Phoebe said.

Everyone looked at T. L., confused. T. L. looked confused.

"They are also my ancestors," Phoebe said.

"Congratulations, Captain Penn. I'm starting to remember things I've learned long ago. So the father was a warrior, and the son was a peacenik. Whose side are you on?" T. L. said.

Phoebe laughed. "I'm not running from my past, Mr. Barrett! I admire them both, though they indeed were not perfect people. We all have to deal with the reality they've left us, don't we? We all have to improve on their mistakes, try to make the world a better place as best we can!" Phoebe said.

"So these great men are your grand-folks, and you're the captain of this costly high-tech ship, and you're telling me that all you're looking for are sunken items from cruise ships, right?" T. L. said.

Phoebe looked at T. L. seriously. "Do you want to dive, Mr. Barrett?" Phoebe said.

"Dive?" T. L. asked.

Phoebe pointed to the minisub that's shaped like a stingray fish. "Yeah, on the *Stingray*," Phoebe said.

"I don't know," T. L. said.

"Don't tell us you're afraid of sharks," Sidney said.

The sub dove with Phoebe, Sidney, and T. L. in it. It had large portal windows and an extensive control panel. "Terry, you're about to see something amazing. Over three hundred years ago, there was a battle in this cove between pirates and Jamaican warriors. Many lost their lives!" Phoebe said.

"Yes, the Battle at Kata Cove," T. L. said.

"That's right, but did you know that the ruins of that battle are still here? Behold, Davy Jones's Locker Room!" Phoebe said.

The sub came to a stop where they vividly saw a graveyard of sunken seventeenth-century shipwrecks.

Coming into view was a vast, crusty gold cauldron on the seafloor.

"There it is!" T. L., Sidney, and Phoebe said.

"Outside of Kata Cove, most people think the Kata story is all a fairy tale! No one knows this exists!" Phoebe said.

"Well, thanks to us, that's going to change! Right, Terry?" Sidney said.

"How is this area so well preserved after all these years?" T. L. said.

"It must be enchanted!" Sidney said.

A camera popped out of a hatch on top of the minisub. A flash went off, and it had taken a clear picture of the Cauldron of Gold. "Gotcha!" Phoebe said.

The sub passed by a skeleton under the cauldron. "Look, that skeleton has four gold rings on its fingers!" T. L. said. T. L. saw the skeleton's hand move; it pointed at him. "See! It's Kata! It's Kata, not a fish!" T. L. said.

"See what?" Sidney said.

T. L. fell to the sub floor in convulsions.

"Terry, are you all right? He's freaking out! We must take him up!" Phoebe said.

Chapter 11:

DI BUCCA JAM

Later that night, T. L. was packing his clothes in his suitcase and drinking fish tea. He picked up *The Sun and the Drum* book and began reading to himself. "To contain a duppy ghost, throw red peas at it. Duppy ghosts hate red peas!" T. L. said. Sissy the chef knocked on his bedroom door.

"How'd dat fish tea work for you?" Sissy said.

"It worked great; I feel great! That is the best soup I've ever had!" T. L. said.

"Tank you, Mr. Barrett. Ya want to eat someting else?" Sissy asked.

"No thanks, Sissy, no more food; I'm about to explode! Where is everybody?" T. L. asked.

"Dem went to Kingston to take care of some coffee business and ting. But dem soon come back," Sissy said. Sissy noticed T. L. was packing his clothes. "Are you going somewhere, Mr. Barrett?" Sissy said.

"Yes, I have decided to cut my visit to Jamaica short and head back to Philly in the morning. I have a club opening up, and I have to get back," T. L. said.

"Really? What a shame!" Sissy said.

"I will be meeting with my uncle Wilvo tonight to thank him for the invitation. Of course, thank you and the Sharp family for your hospitality.

I'm going to get my rum on and cut a rug at this party tonight, then cut out of Kata Cove in the morning!" T. L. said.

"Oh, I found a costume for your party! It's a Black Caesar pirate outfit, complete with hat, dagger, earring, and frilly red shirt!" Sissy said. Sissy held up a frilly flaming-red shirt with a plunging neckline.

"OK, um, you know, Sissy, now that I think of it, there is something else from the kitchen I would like you to fix to go for me: red peas," T. L. said.

T. L. pulled up to the Buccaneer and Pirate Pier and Marina on his motorcycle wearing the Black Caesar pirate costume. He was listening to the song "Back Stabbers," by the O'Jays, on his phone, a Philly soul classic. T. L. said to himself, "OK, didn't see any duppies." T. L. took a ziplock bag of mushy red peas from inside his shirt and put it in a compartment under his motorcycle seat and headed into the party.

To the left, T. L. saw an extensive carnival area with a large banner reading WELCOME TO THE BUCCANEER & PIRATE FESTIVAL. He saw a wonderland of pirate-themed carnival rides, including roller coasters, Ferris wheels, and rock-climbing walls. T. L. also saw a giant helium tour balloon and basket tethered next to the main stage. On the balloon were large words that read CROW'S NEST, with a giant picture of a pirate looking through a spyglass. On the pier to the right was a crowded Jamaican dance hall–style party on two sleek yachts owned by Layton Lafontant that were side by side with a party barge between them. The yachts were dressed up to look like pirate ships, complete with Jolly Roger flags. One of them had a fabulous fake pirate crow's nest on top of it, which consisted of a thick pole with a large wooden basket on it and a fat, plastic pirate skeleton sticking out of it.

Everyone was in seventeenth-century pirate and Jamaican costumes. The DJ was Face, playing some old-school reggae, but to Face's dismay, the crowd was unimpressed. Face was now wearing a cast on his arm and a neck brace as a result of the Jet Ski accident he had earlier. T. L. acknowledged Face and chuckled, as he knew he was in trouble with the crowd.

Face yelled to T. L. on his microphone, "Yo, Yankee man, you tink you got someting better den me?" The crowd turned to T. L., who pulled out his phone, which had some of the latest hits on it. He walked up to the

DJ booth and plugged the phone into the mixer. The crowd immediately approved and danced to the music.

Face was pissed off. "You not gettin' no title round here, Yankee Raise! It's mi who run tings! You nah see it?" Face said.

"Where's my uncle Wilvo?" T. L. asked. Face ignored T. L.'s question.

An attractive hostess wearing a sexy pirate outfit walked up to Face and smacked him in the back of his head. "Ya need to get some new mixes! Mi likkle brodda, him a spoil brat! Dr. Barrett, I presume?" Mia said.

"Well, my parents always wanted me to be one," T. L. said.

"Hi, mi Mia Gettens. I was told to treat ya special," Mia said.

"Please start the treatment!" T. L. said.

"Ya uncle Wilvo? Oh, him tied up right now. Him hasn't call ya cause him lost him phone," Mia said.

"He lost his phone again?" T. L. asked.

"Relax, mon! Come wit mi!" Mia demanded.

Outside, the party crowd was shocked and amazed as they watched Lady Crawlene, the duppy ghost Kriplin, and three other duppies arrive— one was carrying its head—at the party and walk in procession toward the yachts. The crowd applauded, as they thought they were part of the seventeenth-century masquerade.

Inside, Mia led T. L. to Layton Lafontant, the gangster and modern-day pirate leader. Layton was decked out in a French pirate outfit, complete with a dramatic puffy white wig. "Terry Lee Love, mi like to introduce ya ta a mon dat ya should become terrific friends wit, the illustrious Mr. Layton Lafontant!" Mia said.

"Layton Lafontant. Is there an ointment for that?" T. L. said.

"Are ya sayin' mi name's funny? Ya wan meet mi likkle friend?" Layton said.

"No need to go there, brotha. I've never heard a name like that, Lafontant. Is that French?" T. L. asked.

"Yes, mi modda dated a French millionaire. Mi neva like him, may him rest in pieces. But di girls seem to like mi last name, so mi kep it," Layton said.

"You must be truly blessed; look at all this," T. L. said.

"Tell mi, DJ Terry Love, di Jamerican in Charge, have you ever tought bout buildin' a pier on ya fadda's land?" Layton said.

"A pier? For what?" T. L. asked.

"Wha' ya mean, fa wha'? Ta bring up all dat gold, mon!" Layton said.

Mia laughed, and Morgan Gritch walked up. "Gritch!" Layton said.

"Hey, look who's here! Barrett the privateer! Philly in the house!" Gritch said.

"Hey, governor, thanks for the invite. Still in your same funky pirate outfit? What are we going to do with you?" T. L. said.

"Let's throw him over di side!" Layton taunted.

"What?" T. L. said.

"Let's toss him! No one gwan come lookin', and dey wouldn't find him anyway!" Layton said. Layton laughed and was given a microphone. "Now, mi would like five ladies to meet our special guest from Philly, Mr. DJ Terry Love, in person!" Layton said. Five hired girls ran up to T. L. on cue.

"You're kidding, right?" T. L. said.

"What's wrong, are ya savin' yaself for someone? Someone we all know, maybe? Stick around, ladies, Mr. Love will be back soon! Your uncle Wilvo is down here," Layton said. Layton signaled to his security guards, and they hustled T. L. down the hall into a conference room. A pissed-off Morgan Gritch pulled Layton to the side.

"You embarrass me like that in front of that little wanker Barrett again, and you'll see what you get!" Gritch said.

"Now, now, ya sensitive marauder, remember who pays ya bills!" Layton said. Gritch pointed to pictures of historical buccaneers and pirates on a wall. He put his finger on a picture of the famed pirate Henry Morgan.

"Hey, you! The people are coming to the Buccaneer and Pirate Festival to see Captain Morgan; that's me!" Gritch said. Gritch then put his finger on a picture of the famed French buccaneer Jean Baptiste du Casse. "They're not coming to see a phony Jean Baptiste du Casse, and you look nothing like him! You can't, and you're nothing close to being French!" Gritch said. Layton laughed as Gritch stormed down the hall to the conference room.

In the conference room, six dangerous-looking men were standing around the conference table. Gritch started arranging a DVD presentation on a big screen at the head of the table. "Gentleman, our honored guest has arrived; please take ya seats. DJ Terry Love, mi like ya to meet some friends of mine. It's di First Annual Buccaneer and Pirate Festival! We are poised ta shock di world wit a show dat will bring us fame and fortune and make us famous too!" Layton announced.

"Ha, ha, that's funny; I guess there's an echo in here!" T. L. laughed.

"Excuse mi?" Layton said.

"You said it would make us famous twice! A joke, right?" T. L. said. The bad guys looked at T. L. like they wanted to kill him. T. L. slowly took a seat.

"Bind and gag Barrett!" Layton said.

The bad guys tied up T. L. and placed duct tape on his mouth. Layton tossed Gritch a red Magic Marker, and he wrote the word AKATA on the duct tape. All the bad guys laughed. "As I was sayin', we are about to shock di world! Watch dis special presentation," Layton said.

The festival promotion video began to run on a big screen. In it, Gritch was shipside speaking into the camera. "Ahoy mates, this is Captain Morgan Gritch. This weekend's Annual Buccaneer and Pirate Festival will be nothing short of spectacular! With a buccaneer and pirate carnival, top-name entertainment, period swordfights, and the parade of the buccaneer and pirate ships! And wait till ya see the "Crow's Nest"—the helium tour balloon! Don't worry, lassies and laddies, it only goes up four hundred feet, then ya look around, and you come right back down. The event will be a big hit with the kiddies! Why, they'll feel like Captain Morgan himself!"

As everyone was watching the video, Captain Phoebe Penn entered the conference room dressed like William Penn the Quaker. She whispered in Layton's ear. "Sorry I'm late," Phoebe said.

"Mi don't do late! Did ya bring mi di underwata picture of di Cauldron of Gold?" Layton said.

"Yes, here it is," Phoebe said. Phoebe showed Layton the picture of the Cauldron of Gold. Phoebe slipped into a seat next to T. L., and she was shocked to see him tied up. Phoebe whispered to T. L., "Boy, is Layton acting weird. Hey, that's a great costume. All tied up, huh? Don't tell me, you're playing a hostage, right?"

The video presentation stopped, and the lights came on. "OK men, di evidence is in, and we all know why we are really here! Captain Penn, hold up dat picture!" Layton said. Phoebe held up the picture of the cauldron for all to see.

"We intend to bring up di Cauldron of Gold from di bottom of Kata Cove tomorrow at noon! It's di perfect time because everyone in di parish will be right here at Bucca Pier for di Buccaneer and Pirate Festival. We now know as a result of dis picture dat di cauldron is actually down dere, and di only people who know about it are in dis room," Layton said.

"Well, there is one other who knows about it, sir," Gritch said.

"You mean Lady Crawlene Sands? Dat witch will be done away wit soon enough!" Layton said.

"Excuse me, Mr. Lafontant, you cannot disturb that area at Kata Cove! I intend to make it an official archaeological site, and we would need Mr. Barrett's permission to do so. His family owns the whole cove, both land and sea. I haven't discussed it with him yet," Phoebe said.

Everyone stared at T. L., who was looking outside the conference room window and was stunned to see the duppy ghost Kriplin standing outside the door. The conference door flew open, and one of Layton's security guards was thrown into the room. A parrot wearing a micro–video camera on its head flew into the room. Crawlene, standing in the passageway, was watching her cell phone screen. The video camera on the parrot's head made it possible for her to see what was happening in the yacht confer-ence room. The three other duppies were standing behind Crawlene and watching. Kriplin entered.

"Kriplin is here! Kriplin is here!" the parrot said. Layton's bad men pulled swords. Kriplin grabbed Layton and put a machete to his throat. Kriplin, in his brutish British accent, said, "Ahoy, Terry Love! Gimmie the picture of the Cauldron of Gold! I will take it to Lady Crawlene!" Everyone looked at each other in disbelief.

Phoebe whispered to T. L., "Your friend appears to be in a hypnotic state." T. L. moaned under his taped mouth. Phoebe pulled off the tape and put it on his backpack. "I've heard of authentic costumes, but come on. Maybe you should talk to him before he hurts somebody?" Phoebe said.

"Can't you see—I'm a hostage!" T. L. said.

"I know, and I'm portraying William Penn the Quaker. Now, who's that guy?" Phoebe said.

Kriplin threw T. L. a machete, and he caught it. "Didn't you say my family owns the whole cove, land and sea too?" T. L. asked.

"Yes," Phoebe said.

"Then, that picture of the Cauldron of Gold belongs to me, right?"

"Right," Phoebe said. Phoebe took the machete and chops T. L.'s ropes, releasing him. Phoebe handed the picture to T. L., and he put it in his pocket.

In the passageway, Crawlene was watching her phone and then heard an announcer from the stage. The announcer said, "And now it's time for di Queen of di Dance Hall competition finals!" A crowd of women ran down the passageway, forcing Crawlene and her duppy ghost entourage to move with the crowd to the party barge dance floor.

Inside the conference room, Layton was negotiating his release from Kriplin's grip. "Look, Love, is dis some joke? Do you like pictures? Do you want to take mi picture? Tell your smelly friend to put down him machete, and ya take mi picture! Mi smilin'!" Layton said.

"This isn't a joke! Now, where is my uncle Wilvo?" T. L. said.

Phoebe took out her phone. "I'll take the darn picture!" Phoebe said. Phoebe snapped a picture, and the flash blinded Kriplin.

Layton elbowed Kriplin in the gut, and the commotion began. "Get Barrett! Get him!" Layton said.

Phoebe crawled under the table. "Nothing personal, but I'm a pacifist, not a warrior. I'll see you later, Mr. Barrett!" Phoebe said. Phoebe opened a hatch on the floor and escaped through it. She landed in the belly of the yacht filled with barrels of stolen Sharp Jamaican Coffee. "Oh, no! Modern-day pirates!" Phoebe said. Phoebe snapped pictures. Phoebe heard moaning behind a barrel of coffee and saw Uncle Wilvo tied up and gagged. Phoebe removed his gag.

"Captain Penn!" Uncle Wilvo said.

"Mr. Wilvo?" Phoebe said.

Up in the conference room, T. L. was now facilitating his escape, attempting to fight off multiple bad guys.

On the party dance floor, Crawlene was now competing in di Queen of di Dance Hall contest with spectacular dance moves, to the crowd's delight. She glanced at her phone and saw the commotion going on in the conference room. Crawlene grabbed the microphone out of the announcer's hand. "Kriplin, possess Mr. Barrett! Yah hear mi? Possess him and fight dem!" Lady Crawlene said. The crowd was shocked and frightened.

In the conference room, Kriplin heard Crawlene's plea and ran toward T. L., disappearing into him. T. L. "hulked up," growing three times his size with large, protruding muscles. "I'm pumpin' up the volume past level 11!" possessed T. L. said. He exhibited incredible sword skills and a fantastic power wave emanated from the palms of his hands. His assailants ran in fear as he strutted through the room. "I'm pumpin' up the volume to level *possessed*!" possessed T. L. said.

T. L. punched a hole in the yacht wall and walked onto the side of the ship. He walked by a tiki torch, and his tattered pants caught on fire. T. L. ran down the gangway. "Whoa, ow, ow, ow!" possessed T. L. said.

The fire caused Kriplin to leave T. L.'s body, and T. L. returned to his average size. His pants were still on fire, and he jumped off the yacht and into the water. A bad guy came around the corner and attempted to harpoon T. L., but the bad guy got knocked out by Taino's sudden appearance. "It's Taino time!" Taino said. Taino was duly adorned for the costume party, wearing only a loincloth and a traditional Taino feathered headdress.

T. L. swam to shore and stumbled down the road. Phoebe, helping Uncle Wilvo, bumped into T. L. "Oops, sorry!" Phoebe said.

"Uncle Wilvo, are you all right? What are you two mixed up in here?" T. L. said.

"Us? It's you and your spooky friend they seem to want! Listen, I'd talk more, but I gotta get to Montego Bay in the morning to pick up something that you must see!" Phoebe said. Phoebe ran off.

Imani turned Taino's limo headlights on T. L., Uncle Wilvo, and Taino. Imani yelled out the window, "I'm not even going to ask what happened!" Trotting toward the limo were the three other duppies that were with Lady Crawlene. "Hurry up; get in the limo!" Imani said.

T. L. ran to his motorcycle and grabbed the bag of red peas. They all got in the limo. A duppy ghost jumped onto the hood of the limo, and Taino pressed on the gas pedal. They sped down the road.

"Hey, where ya gwan! Lady Crawlene wants di picture of di Cauldron of Gold! Remember di deal she made wit you!" the duppy ghost said.

T. L. opened the sunroof and threw the messy red peas at the duppy ghost, smacking it in the face. "Deal with that!" T. L. said. The duppy ghost shrieked and exploded.

"Thanks, Imani and Taino! You guys saved our butts! What is happening? I don't know whether to be scared or excited that I seem to have superpowers!" T. L. said.

"Dat was scary when di light wave came out of your hands!" Taino said.

"What?" Imani said.

"Uncle Wilvo, those guys are trying to take my family and my ancestral legacy from me, right in front of my face! We're going to have to call the police!" T. L. said.

"Dat we will not do! Our family has defended Kata Cove without di police for hundreds of years! Dey would bring di army and di air force, and dey would fail!" Uncle Wilvo said.

"Well, what will you have me do?" T. L. said.

"Di only ting dat can stop di duppy ghost apocalypse is you taking Kata's magic sword, di Iron Thorn, and…" Uncle Wilvo said.

"And what?" T. L. said.

"And di rest your father will tell you! Drive to the Barrett House. Taino, step 'pon it!" Uncle Wilvo said.

Chapter 12:

THE IRON THORN

The limo pulled up to the Barrett House. They all followed Uncle Wilvo to the old well behind the house. "What are we doing?" Imani said.

"Taino, will you please assist Terry in removing dose rocks from on top of di well?" Uncle Wilvo said.

"Dem boulders are big, mon!" Taino said.

"Dat's why he's going to need a hand!" Uncle Wilvo said.

Uncle Wilvo lighted tiki torches. T. L. and Taino took off the boulders covering the well. Uncle Wilvo unlocked the wooden lid and opened it. There was a long ladder going down into the darkness. "I'm too old, but our destiny and our ability to continue to live here are in dat well. Di Iron Thorn is down dere!" Uncle Wilvo said.

"I'm going down there. Will you wait for me?" T. L. said to Imani.

"Ya, mon, mi wait fa yah!" Taino said.

"I was talking to Imani!" T. L. said.

"Taino, go with him!" Imani said.

"I should stand guard and protect Uncle Wilvo!" Taino said.

"OK, you stand guard! I'll go with you, Terry!" Imani said.

Uncle Wilvo handed T. L. and Imani the tiki torches. T. L. and Imani went down into the well. They walked through an eerie tunnel and came to a large ornate door with African symbols on it. T. L. opened the door, and before them was the Kata warrior shrine and Dr. Barrett's library and study filled with historical artifacts. T. L. took Imani's tiki torch and put it in a torch holder. They walked to the center of the shrine.

T. L. saw a youthful picture of his parents on a large desk. "Love you, Mom and Dad. I miss you," T. L. said.

"We miss you too, Terry," Mrs. Barrett's ghost said. He looked around for his mother but saw nothing.

"Did you hear someone?" T. L. said.

"No! Now you're trying to scare mi?" Imani said.

He saw a small burlap bag with a drawstring on the desk. He opened the bag and saw incredibly shiny pebbles of gold. "This looks like gold!" T. L. said.

"The Ashanti gold of the Kata legend!" Imani said.

He poured some Ashanti gold in an envelope and gave it to Imani, then put the bag in his pocket.

Imani picked up an old leather-bound book. "Look, I think I found a diary!" Imani said.

"That's great, my father's diary!" T. L. said. He saw a mirror reflection of his mother. His mother looked angelic, wearing a radiant gown. She pointed to Empress Iyadola's bejeweled magic necklace and wristband on a pedestal next to the mirror. T. L. noticed that the wristband was made of iron with a golden lion emblazoned on it. Imani could not see or hear Mrs. Barrett's ghost speak.

"Give the Empress Iyadola's magic necklace and wristband to Imani," Mrs. Barrett's ghost said in her American accent.

"Mom?" T. L. said.

"What?" Imani said.

His mother's ghost disappeared. T. L. put his tiki torch in another torch holder. He walked over to the pedestal and picked up Empress Iyadola's magic necklace and wristband. "These are for you," T. L. said.

"Empress Iyadola's magic necklace and wristband! They're beautiful!" Imani said.

"My mother wanted you to have them," T. L. said.

"Your mother?" Imani said. Imani put them on and looked at herself in the mirror. Behind her, she saw Empress Iyadola's Magic Golden Abeng. She ran over to it. "Terry, this is Empress Iyadola's Magic Golden Abeng! It is said that if you blow it twice, her ferocious alligator friend named Blacka will appear and do di worst!" Imani said.

"An alligator friend named Blacka?" T. L. responded in disbelief.

Suddenly, the tiki torch blew out. "I'll get the other torch," Imani said. Imani walked across the room and saw a sizable ancient-looking book on a stand entitled *The Book of Ancient African Alchemy*. Imani started leafing through the mysterious book.

Meanwhile, T. L. saw a life-size mold of a left and a right hand on a futuristic-looking podium with a 3D sign on it that said, 'Believe In the Planet Earth!' When T. L. got close to it, a foot-high 3D holographic message popped up with a man wearing a metallic visor and what looked like a pimped-out spacesuit. He said, "This is Roland Hawk. Thank you, Dr. Barrett, for all your help. It is official; you may keep the Ten Golden Rings of Walatah. Continue to use these extraordinary rings wisely, and continue to believe in the planet earth!"

There was one Kata magic ring left on the mold. He took it off and put it on his finger. He now had three rings on his hand. "Are these rings from outer space or something?" T. L. said to himself.

T. L. turned and saw a stunning-looking African kente-cloth curtain hanging on the wall. T. L. walked over to the wall and pulled the curtain drawstring. The curtain opened to reveal a large sword in an ornate African sheath on the wall: the Iron Thorn.

He took the sword off the wall and out of its sheath. The Iron Thorn was a lethal-looking weapon; it was three feet long with a five-inch iron blade at its neck, and it arced out to ten inches at its fullest. The hilt was made of two golden balls with a six-inch handle between the balls. T. L. saw a reflection of his father and mother in a large mirror.

"Son, I'm sorry. Again, I wanted to keep the Kata story a secret. You will now have to do what I should have done years ago," Dr. Barrett's duppy ghost said.

"Huh, Dad? What's that, Dad?" a frightened T. L. said.

"Destroy the Iron Thorn! Show Kata Cove that you represent the power of love!" Dr. Barrett's duppy ghost said.

"The power of love?" T. L. said.

"Hear mi, son. Kata used the extreme ancestral powers of sorcery to create the Iron Thorn and fight against unspeakable oppression! Slavery in the Caribbean was an evil, brutal, inhumane institution that Kata would not bow to! He would never remain enslaved! However, now, Kata's old weapons are too dangerous! They attract hostility, not peace, and they must go! Terry Lee, smash dat Iron Thorn into pieces!" Dr. Barrett's duppy ghost said.

"Hmmm. But, Dad, it's Kata's historic sword we would destroy! A sword fit for a superhero, right? And this sword has got to be worth a fortune! It's made of gold too!" T. L. said.

"When it's the end, we can't take any of our gold with us, Terry! And you have a long life ahead of you, we hope. As I've always taught you, your job here on earth is to work at living in peace with everyone and live a holy life!" Dr. Barrett's duppy ghost said.

"You're right, Dad! I am a peaceful guy, and I try to make people happy too! Dad, we could educate a lot of people and pay a lot of bills if we start a museum!" T. L. said.

"People steal from museums, Terry! And then you are going to want to start using that sword against people who bother you! War is not the answer! Times have changed, son. History has proven to us that the new and righteous way to fight against those who oppress us is through the use of nonviolence. Beware of greed; it's a bottomless pit! Destroy the sword now! When the Iron Thorn is destroyed, its pursuers will fly away," Dr. Barrett's duppy ghost said.

"Fly away? Really, Dad? Like birds, Dad?" T. L. chuckled.

Dr. Barrett pointed to Kata's Golden Sledgehammer on the wall. "There is Kata's Sledgehammer, the only ting that can destroy the Iron Thorn, and you're the only person who can destroy it!" Dr. Barrett's duppy ghost said.

"Of course, Dad, I will do what you say! Um, Dad, could you give me a day or two to destroy the sword? I have my friend Imani here, and I don't want her to think I'm crazy by bashing this famous and beautiful sword into pieces," T. L. said.

"Just as I thought, you will have to learn for yourself and on your own! When you get around to destroying the sword, pour the Ashanti gold that's in your pocket on the sword first. Just in case," Dr. Barrett's duppy ghost said.

"Just in case of what, Dad?" T. L. said.

"It's di last ting to do, Terry Lee!" Dr. Barrett's ghost yelled.

"The last thing to do? Hey, Dad, why didn't you destroy the Iron Thorn when you had the chance?" T. L. said.

"Why didn't you finish college instead of dropping out and becoming a record player?" Dr. Barrett's duppy ghost retorted.

"Oh, honey, he's a deejay. An artist," Mrs. Barrett's ghost said.

"What? He plays records; that's not an artist! Pure foolishness! OK, we love you, Terry, and it's time to leave you now. Make your parents proud, and do what I told you to do!" Dr. Barrett's duppy ghost said.

T. L.'s parents disappeared, which created a stiff breeze. The breeze blew a sheet off a mannequin with Kata's African king's crown and vest on it. "Wait, Dad! I've been seeing someone walking around in this crown and vest lately! Is that you?" T. L. said.

There was no answer from Dr. Barrett. T. L. laid the Iron Thorn on an African chair. He walked over to Imani.

"Terry, are you all right? You're talking to yourself, sweetheart. Now, I know this is a lot for you," Imani said.

T. L. took the new-found Kata Magic Ring off his finger and put it on Imani's finger. "Wow, are you proposing? Oh my, this is another one of Kata's Magic Golden Rings. They say if you turn it twice counterclockwise, you can travel through time. Have you tried it yet?" Imani said.

T. L. turned Imani toward the Iron Thorn. "There it is!" T. L. said.
"What?" Imani said.

"The Iron Thorn! It's not just an old ghost story! It's all true! Imani, my father told me to do something to the Iron Thorn," T. L. said. As soon as T. L. repeated the words "Iron Thorn," the sword leaped from the chair and flew directly toward T. L. and Imani. T. L. and Imani screamed. The sword floated before them in midair with the tip of the sword blade pointing at them. "What do you want?" T. L. asked the Thorn.

"Say the magic words, Terry!" Imani said.

"Huh?" T. L. said.

"Say, 'Iron Thorn, mi command you to mi hand!' Hurry up!" Imani said.

"*Iron Thorn, mi command you to mi hand!*" T. L. said. The sword leaped into his hand.

"I told you! You are the new Kata!" Imani said.

T. L. raised the Iron Thorn. "I am the new Kata, the king and the protector!" T. L. said.

"Yes, you are!" Imani said as she hugged T. L.

Outside, Taino noticed Ackee the parrot in a tree. Ackee was wearing the camera on its head. Taino aimed his slingshot at a mango right next to Ackee. "Listen, parrot, mi believe in being kind to animals, but ya gwan have to leave! Here's a warnin' shot!" Taino said. Ackee dive-bombed Taino, and he fell to the ground.

Ackee then flew down into the well. Lady Crawlene was now on the Barrett property watching her phone monitor and getting a clear picture of the Iron Thorn's discovery. "Di Thorn has been in dat well di whole time?" Lady Crawlene said. Lady Crawlene raised her arms and disappeared in a cloud of purple smoke. She reappeared at the bottom of the well next to Ackee. Lady Crawlene produced a Jamaican Anansi spider from a pouch. She took magic sand from another pouch and sprinkled it on the spider. "Anansi, mi mighty spida, bring mi di Iron Thorn!" Lady Crawlene said.

In the Kata shrine room, Imani and T. L. were packing the duffel bag with artifacts and the Iron Thorn. Imani saw Kata's sledgehammer on the wall. "Wow, look at dat sledgehammer!" Imani said.

"Oh, yeah, we'll need that," T. L. said.

As they walked toward the sledgehammer, the ground shook. They pointed their torches backward, and they saw a giant twenty-foot-tall spider emerging from the tunnel. "What on earth is dat!" Imani said.

"Let's see; it's, um, a gigantic spider?" T. L. said.

"Spiders don't grow dat big!" Imani said.

"Apparently, it doesn't know that!" T. L. said. T. L. dropped the duffel bag; then he and Imani ran to the cave wall. Imani saw the Magic Golden Abeng sticking out of the bag, but it was way beyond her reach to call for Blacka the alligator.

"Use di Iron Thorn, Terry! Command it to nyaka-nyaka!" Imani said.

"Good idea! *Iron Thorn, mi command you to nyaka-nyaka the spider!*" T. L. said. The sword, now in its sheath, did not respond.

"What's wrong?" Imani said.

"I don't know; it's not responding! *Iron Thorn, nyaka!*" T. L. said.

"Maybe when it's in the sheath, it won't respond!" Imani said.

The spider advanced closer with its dripping saliva. T. L. threw a rock, but the spider swiftly knocked it away. There was a loud pinging sound off the cave wall, and the spider turned around. Taino had arrived with his slingshot and distracted the spider. Taino tried to fend off the spider with a tiki torch. The spider knocked the torch across the room, and it started a fire. T. L. tried to run under the spider's legs, but he was webbed against the wall. Imani threw another rock, and the spider webbed Imani to the wall next to T. L.

The spider attempted to bite Taino, but he grabbed its fangs and held them apart. With his foot, Taino kicked the Iron Thorn out of its sheath. "Now, Terry!" Imani said.

"*Iron Thorn, kill the spider!*" T. L. said.

"The mighty Kata strikes again? Remember, you have to command it to nyaka-nyaka!" Imani said.

T. L. responded with the magic words: "Iron Thorn, mi command you to nyaka-nyaka the spider!"

Now the Iron Thorn flew up, positioned itself in front of the spider, and forcefully stabbed it right between its multiple eyes. It fell dead with a final ground-shaking thud. The Iron Thorn then moved menacingly toward T. L., Imani, and Taino. "Terry, tell it to cease and sekkle!" Imani said.

"Iron Thorn, cease and settle!" T. L. said.

"Not settle! Sekkle! It's Jamaican patois for the word *settle*!" Imani said.

"Iron Thorn, mi command you to cease and sekkle!" T. L. said. The Iron Thorn halted in midair.

"Iron Thorn, mi command you to mi hand!" T. L. said. The sword leaped into T. L.'s hand. "Spiders? Ha, just bugs!" T. L. exclaimed.

Taino rushed to assist Imani and T. L. out of their webbing.

Lady Crawlene, who had been watching in the shadows, disappeared.

Chapter 13:

DI GREAT ESCAPE

Back at the Sharp Mansion, Captain Ridge and his policemen were questioning Mr. and Mrs. Sharp and Sissy the chef. "Well, I want to talk to Mr. Barrett immediately!" Captain Ridge said.

"What seems to be the problem, Captain?" Mr. Sharp said.

"We hear dat he was in a bad fight!" Captain Ridge said.

"A fight?" Mrs. Sharp said.

"It's been alleged dat he went to the Bucca Jam Party with a sword! He started chasing people around and scared a number of dem badly when him large up, becoming tree times his size!" Captain Ridge said.

"Sword? I didn't see him with any sword in this house! And what do you mean, him large up, becoming tree times his size?" Mr. Sharp said.

"Oh lord, him say he was going to get his rum on and den cut a rug! And I was told by relatives dat him father, Dr. Barrett, researched obeah, witchcraft, and ting! Terry must be possessed too!" Sissy said.

In the Sharps' guest bedroom, Crawlene's parrots, Ackee and Salt, had arrived. Ackee was next to Mrs. Sharp's jewelry box. It grabbed a diamond necklace in its beak and flew down the hall into T. L.'s guest room. In T. L.'s guest room, Ackee opened a side pouch on T. L.'s backpack, put the diamond necklace in, and then zipped it shut. Salt noticed the autographed supermodel magazine with Greta on the cover. Salt tore the cover off the magazine and flew out the window with it. Ackee remained behind.

At the Sharp Mansion back door, T. L., Imani, and Taino sneaked into the kitchen. Taino saw food and stayed in the kitchen. A policeman entered the kitchen and surprised Taino. "Wha' happenin', Taino? Where ya friends?" the policeman said.

In T. L.'s guest room, T. L. was packing his things, including the Iron Thorn. He put the small bag of Ashanti gold next to his backpack. Ackee quickly grabbed the bag and flew out the window undetected. T. L. slung the bamboo briefcase over his shoulder, and Imani slung the Magic Golden Abeng over her shoulder. She pointed to the window. T. L. and Imani ran across the lawn. Captain Ridge and the other policemen saw them running to a motorcycle. "Arrest dem!" Captain Ridge said.

Speeding away on the motorcycle, Imani and T. L. stayed one step ahead of the police. Up ahead was a Y-intersection in the road. Standing in the middle of the Y-intersection was Lady Crawlene Sands and Kriplin sitting on top of a Ten-Eyed Maggoty Bull. Imani and T. L. go right, and Kriplin, riding the Ten-Eyed Maggoty Bull, chased them. The police saw Lady Crawlene Sands and swerved to the left. The Ten-Eyed Maggoty Bull didn't gallop; instead, it floated spookily at a fast clip. "Imani, didn't Kata kill the Ten-Eyed Maggoty Bull?" T. L. said.

"Yes, but it had a son!" Imani said.

T. L. flipped around on the motorcycle seat facing the Bull. He took the Iron Thorn, swung it, and cut the Bull's head off. The rest of the Bull hit the dirt, and Kriplin was thrown from the Bull toward T. L. He tried to grab T. L. but only managed to grab the strap of the bamboo briefcase. The strap broke, and Kriplin and the bamboo briefcase fell down a steep gulch into the darkness. Imani and T. L. rode to the Sharp Airfield by the sea. T. L. and Imani ran to her docked seaplane.

"Wait, we have to find my father's bamboo briefcase!" T. L. said.

"Bad idea, the police are coming to arrest us! I'm gonna fly you to the Montego Bay Airport and get you a ticket to Miami," Imani said.

"What? I can kill those duppies with red peas and the Iron Thorn!" T. L. said.

They heard and saw the policemen's motorcycles coming. "Terry, the duppies aren't your problem right now; the Jamaican police are!" Imani said.

"You're right, anything you say!" T. L. said. T. L. and Imani got into her docked seaplane and took off for Montego Bay.

A breathtaking view of the Jamaican shoreline was visible as the sun came up. Imani spoke to the Montego Bay airport tower on her plane radio. "This is Hummingbird…over! Am I cleared for landing? Over," Imani said. Imani and T. L. saw a line of police cars driving onto the runway. "This looks bad!" Imani said. "They must know about the sword too!" T. L. said.

"I'm gonna have to hide you out until I can get you to a friend of mine who has a private jet service to Miami," Imani said.

Imani and T. L. flew away from the airport and landed on the water by a small uninhabited island. They walked to a bamboo lean-to. Imani opened a minirefrigerator with a solar panel on top. "Solar electricity!" Imani said. The fridge had "Ting" sodas in it, a popular Jamaican beverage. "Still cold. Would you like a Ting?" Imani asked.

"Um, Imani, this is not the Ting that's mentioned in the Kata stories, is it?" T. L. said.

"No, dis Ting is not dat Ting! And I don't want to talk about dat Ting! This is my island getaway. So how come a cute guy like you isn't married?" Imani said.

"I'm a struggling artist, Imani. You know that deejays are artists too. But romance without finance is a nuisance! I've finally saved up enough money to start my own club in Philly. It opens in two weeks. Hopefully, I'll make enough to start a family. And you? Why aren't you hitched?" T. L. said.

"Time flies, you know, helping my folks with the coffee company and working at the school. And I've been waiting for the right guy. I've never been much of a party girl. I guess most men find mi boring," Imani said.

"Boring? I get excited just thinking about you," T. L. said. T. L. pulled Imani close, and they kissed.

"I believe that coming back to Kata Cove was really meant for me to meet you again, I've always been in love with you, Imani!" T. L. said.

"Oh, Terry, that is the most beautiful thing that you could say to me," Imani said. Imani started to cry and hugged T. L.

"I need to take care of your jet tickets to get you back to the States! Where's your passport?" Imani said.

"I got it right there in my backpack," T. L. said. Imani looked in T. L.'s backpack and grabbed his passport. She didn't notice her mother's diamond necklace. "Terry, my love, please bury that sword!" Imani said.

"It will be done, sweetheart!" T. L. said. Imani flew away.

Chapter 14:

GRETA'S RETURN

T. L. went to his backpack and took out a piece of one of Lady Crawlene's cookies and bit into it. "The last piece left of Lady Crawlene's cookie," T. L. said. T. L. saw a coconut in a tree. "Iron Thorn, mi command you to nyaka-nyaka the coconut!" T. L. said. The Iron Thorn not only cut the coconut from the tree, but it also sliced the top off and served it to T. L. on its blade. "Can you think on your own? 'Cause I didn't ask you to chop the top of this coconut off and serve it up like a butler!" T. L. said. The Iron Thorn hovered in the air. The sword's tip was pointing directly at T. L.'s heart. The sight was alarming, and T. L. had a vision:

The Iron Thorn hovered in the air with its tip pointing at T. L.'s heart. The Iron Thorn suddenly stabbed T. L. in the chest, and he fell to his knees. T. L. was twirling in deep space and heard and saw his father's ghost tell him, "Beware of greed! Destroy di sword!" He then saw Imani's still body underwater. She helplessly floated away, appearing dead.

T. L. came out of the vision in shock. He checked his body for a stab wound; there wasn't one. The Iron Thorn still hovered in the air in front of him with the sword's tip pointing at his heart.

"I think this island is going to be your final resting place, pal! *Iron Thorn, mi command you to mi hand!*" T. L. said. The Iron Thorn didn't move. It still hovered in the air in front of him with the sword's tip pointing at his heart. T. L. was shocked and scared and repeated the request. "Iron Thorn, mi command you to mi hand!" T. L. said.

The sword slowly returned into T. L.'s hand. He put it in its sheath and dropped it on the sand. "Bad sword! Bad, bad sword!" T. L. said. T. L. heard a scream out at sea. He took his pirate spyglass, looked, and saw Greta, the supermodel whom he met on the Caribbean Air jet, on a raft, waving at him. "Hey, mon! Help! Please, help mi!" Greta said in a strong Jamaican accent.

T. L. ran to the water's edge. "Come on; I'll grab you!" T. L. said. Greta took her bamboo pole and pushed herself toward T. L. She fell on top of him, and they landed on the beach. "Oh, tyank yu!" Greta said.

"What happened?" T. L. said.

"Mi was doin' a phota shoot off di shore of MoBay, and a big wave come in, den di raft broke free. Di current was so fass dat mi float here!" Greta said.

"It's OK; you're all right now! Don't worry; my friend is coming back to get me soon!" T. L. said. T. L. got a towel for Greta and spread a blanket out. "I'll get you some water!" T. L. said.

"Rum is fine. Tyanks. Do you have any lotion?" Greta said.

"Yeah! I'll get it! So Greta, you have been practicing your Jamaican patois! You sound like a real Jamaican now!"

T. L. grabbed some water out of the fridge and a bottle of sunblock lotion out of his backpack. In his backpack, he noticed the cover of the supermodel magazine that Greta autographed had been removed. *Who ripped that off?* T. L. said to himself. "Got the lotion!" T. L. said to Greta.

T. L. was about to put the lotion on Greta's shoulders when the parrot Ackee, sitting above him in a tree, pooped on his forehead. He had to get another towel. "I'll be right back!" T. L. said. T. L. ran back to the lean-to. He wiped his face off, grabbed the Iron Thorn, and looked for the parrot.

He heard a boat motor off in the distance. T. L. dropped the Iron Thorn and ran to get his spyglass. "Oh, dat must be mi ride!" Greta said. From the lens of the spyglass, T. L. could see who was operating the boat. It was Kriplin, the duppy ghost in a long-hooded raincoat. "Oh no, is that

Kriplin? Greta, I don't want anyone to know I'm here! Wait a minute, do you know this guy?" T. L. said.

Greta kissed T. L. then pushed him, and he fell. "Ya sit tight; mi meet him out in di wata," Greta said. T. L. watched Greta getting in the boat with Kriplin, and they rode off. T. L. saw Greta morph into Crawlene the witch right before his eyes. He looked to Crawlene's right, and he saw the stolen Iron Thorn in the boat. "What the hey? You thievin' witch! I'm going to get you, Crawlene!" T. L. yelled. A coconut came down on T. L.'s head, courtesy of Crawlene's parrot. T. L. was knocked out.

Chapter 15:

POLICE, THIEVES, AND PHOEBE IN THE STREETS

At the Montego Bay airport, Phoebe was in line in the airport package pickup room. Police officers were watching her from across the room and looking at Phoebe's pictures in their hands. Phoebe walked up to a package assistant's window.

"Can I help you, ma'am?" the package assistant said.

"Yes, I'm Captain Phoebe Penn. Here is my ID. I'm here to pick up a package," Phoebe said.

The package assistant gave Phoebe a ticket. "Please have a seat, Captain Penn; your package will be out momentarily," the package assistant said. Phoebe turned to sit down and got a phone call. It was Imani. "Imani Sharp, how are you?" Phoebe said.

Outside, Morgan Gritch was also at the MoBay airport, picking up festival artists in a limousine. Gritch saw Phoebe walking to her Jeep with her package. Phoebe pulled away from the curb. Gritch quickly followed. The police were also trailing Phoebe and follow her in an unmarked car.

Chapter 16:

IMANI VEX

Meanwhile, Imani arrived back on her getaway island in her plane and saw T. L. knocked out. Imani doused his face with water, awakening him. "It's Imani! Are you still alive?" Imani said.

"Ooh, my head," T. L. said.

"What happened to you?" Imani said.

"I think a coconut fell off the tree and got me good," T. L. said.

"My parents are asking a lot of questions about you!" Imani said.

Imani saw a beach blanket, suntan lotion, female sunglasses, and a scarf. "Did you have company, or do you like fancy eyewear?" Imani said.

"Let me tell you what happened. That witch I told you about? It was her! She was here, and oh, you're not gonna believe this!" T. L. said.

"Try mi!" Imani said.

"She stole the Iron Thorn!" T. L. said.

"The old witch?" Imani said.

"Yes, Lady Crawlene is her name!" T. L. said.

"Was she wearing a scarf?" Imani said.

"Well, when she was the supermodel, she was. You see, she snuck in here as a supermodel first. Then she turned into the witch! I know it sounds incredible, but so was the big spider in the well, right? You saw that with your own eyes! And what about the duppy ghosts we saw on the road!" T. L. said.

"The duppy ghosts, Terry? They were people dressed up at a costume party! I hear that some people are trying to, quote, 'scare you back to Philly!' They're scaring mi too!" Imani said.

"Well, what do you believe?" T. L. said.

"I believe in the power of love, Terry! Didn't you call yourself DJ Terry Love before you said it wasn't cool anymore? Yes, the power of love, kindness, and compassion toward others! Human decency, dignity, and respect for each other are what I believe in! As a matter of fact, the word *respect* is probably the most spoken and most vital in Jamaica! We say respect to each other every day, all day! And this witch and pirate ting is getting in the way of mi respect for you!" Imani screamed.

Imani started searching through T. L.'s things. "Hey! Imani, those are my personal belongings!" T. L. said.

"I thought you said what's yours is mine!" Imani said.

"Did I? I mean, what of mine do you want to be yours exactly?" T. L. said.

"My mother's diamond necklace, for one thing!" Imani said.

Imani produced her mother's necklace from T. L.'s bag. "I don't know how that got there! I didn't take it!" T. L. said.

"Oh, let's see! The witch did it, right?" Imani said.

T. L. walked toward Imani. "Imani, you're upset, and I understand, but I don't want to lose you!" T. L. said.

Imani produced her slingshot. "Yu vex me now; stay right where ya are! Dis ting hurts, and mi know just how to use it!" Imani said.

"Imani, I'm going to take care of all this! Take me back to Kata Cove!" T. L. said.

"Oh, be quiet! Ever since you got here, nothing but trouble! Just trouble!" Imani said.

"How do you think I feel?" T. L. said.

Imani noticed the supermodel magazine's pages flapping in the breeze. "So what did she look like?" Imani said.

"Who?" T. L. said.

"Lady Crawlene, the witch-supermodel?" Imani said.

"She was ugly and a thief! If you put lipstick on a pig, it's still a pig! She has a pig too," T. L. said.

"Why do you have a supermodel magazine?" Imani said.

"Imani, you see…I met the supermodel on the jet to Jamaica. Her name is Greta," T. L. said.

"You met her *before* today?" Imani said.

"Listen, I believe Lady Crawlene can assume your identity if she has an autographed picture of you! When I first met Lady Crawlene, she wanted me to autograph a picture of myself, but the pen broke before I could do it! Greta autographed the magazine cover and gave it to me! I think Lady Crawlene stole the magazine cover and turned herself into Greta!" T. L. said.

Imani was rubbing her temples in disgust. "I called Phoebe! Lucky for you, she is here in Montego Bay and will meet you at the Damali Beach Pier! She will get you to my friend with the private jet who can fly you back to the US. Let's go!" Imani said. She walked fast toward her plane. T. L. ran after her.

Chapter 17

AKATA

Ten minutes later, Imani and T. L. docked on the water at the Damali Beach Pier. "You gotta believe me; I didn't steal your mom's necklace!" T. L. said.

"I don't know what to believe after these last few days, Terry. Call mi when you get back to the States. I will talk to Captain Ridge and try to get this thing straightened out," Imani said.

"Thanks, Imani, for you and your help. I will see you soon," T. L. said.

On T. L.'s backpack, Imani saw the duct tape with the word *akata* written on it. "Where did you get that?" Imani said.

"The bad guys put this over my mouth when they took me hostage on Layton's yacht last night," T. L. said.

Imani pointed to the word *akata*. "What a difference an *A* makes, huh?" Imani said.

T. L. looked at Imani, confused. "You know what that word means, don't you?" Imani said.

"What, A-Kata?" T. L. said.

"It's not pronounced A-Kata; it's pronounced *ah-kah-tah*. Do you know what it means?" Imani said.

"Huh?" T. L. said.

"The guys at Buccaneer and Pirate Pier use the word *akata* as a derogatory slang word, as an insult to Kata. It's like a put-down to anyone associated with Kata," Imani said.

"Oh yeah? Well, what does the slang, insult, put-down word mean?" T. L. said.

Imani looked away and waved T. L. off, as she did not want to tell him. "Come on, what does it mean?" T. L. said.

"Akata is an African word, and the original definition means 'wildcat,' I think. But now they use it to say something else to describe someone," Imani said.

"Like what?" T. L. said.

"Like a bush animal! The word means bush animal! Or, uh, worse than that!" Imani said.

T. L. was stunned, insulted, and angered by the statement. Imani crumpled the tape and tossed it into her trash can. "They're calling me a bush animal or worse? What a difference an *A* does make, all right!" T. L. said.

"It's ignorant, Terry," Imani said.

"So they want to continue to insult the great Kata, and me too! A Jamaican hero who wouldn't remain enslaved! A man who should be celebrated and respected!" T. L. said.

"Everyone knows about the enormous contribution Jamaicans have made in music, athletics, and education, Terry. It's a few, stupid, ignorant guys like the ones at Buccaneer and Pirate Pier. They want to ignore, forget, and—" Imani said.

"Run from their past!" Imani and T. L. said at the same time.

T. L. looked seriously at Imani. "Yes, what a difference an *A* does make! You're about to see the difference I'm gonna make, Imani! They're gonna learn to respect me!" T. L. said.

T. L. kissed Imani on the cheek, got out of the plane, and walked away. Imani reached into her pocketbook and pulled out Empress Iyadola's magic necklace. She started to cry.

Chapter 18:

BORN TO RUN

Phoebe pulled up to Damali Beach in her Jeep. Morgan Gritch pulled up behind Phoebe's Jeep at a comfortable distance. The police, in an unmarked car, did the same. Phoebe waved to T. L.

"Man, am I glad to see you!" T. L. said.

"Ditto, my friend! So you're leaving the island?" Phoebe said.

"I don't think so! I found the Iron Thorn!" T. L. said.

"Imani told me everything, though very quickly! Where is it?" Phoebe said.

"That's the good news. The bad news is that this witch named Lady Crawlene stole it from me! Lady Crawlene, Morgan Gritch, and Layton Lafontant want to use the Cauldron of Gold and the Iron Thorn to unleash a duppy ghost pirate army and apocalypse and rule the world! All this is supposed to happen tomorrow at noon! I believe I am the only person who can stop it! Also, have you ever heard of something called di Evil Ting?" T. L. said.

"Thankfully, no! Di Evil Ting sounds creepy, man! I'm here to help, but Imani said you were going back to the US!" Phoebe said.

"Hey, Captain Phoebe Olivia Penn, I'm not running from my past! Let's get back to Kata Cove now!" T. L. said.

"That's the spirit, Terry Lee Barrett!" Phoebe said.

Phoebe and T. L. sped off in the Jeep. In the back of the Jeep, unseen, was Ackee the parrot, shooting video. Both Morgan Gritch in his limo and the police followed them, and the chase was on.

Jamaican traffic could be dangerous, and a car chase was the last thing T. L. and Phoebe wanted to encounter. However, T. L. looked in his passenger-side mirror and saw Morgan Gritch with a more crazed than usual look in his eyes, speeding up behind them. He bumped Phoebe's Jeep. The musicians in Gritch's limo were bumping around like pinballs.

"What was that?" Phoebe yelled.

"We got a big problem, Phoebe! That's that nutcase Morgan Gritch, who is working with the witch I told you about to try to steal everything my family owns! You better move it!" T. L. said.

Phoebe put her foot on the gas pedal. "Lucky for us, this brand-new Jeep has a 707-horsepower monster engine in it," Phoebe bragged.

T. L. saw Morgan Gritch's limo fading behind them at a comfortable distance. The road to Rick's Café in Negril suffered ill repair, and the high speed at which the cars were traveling made the chase even more dangerous. The unmarked police car behind Gritch's limo hit a pothole the size of a moon crater that ended their hunt and vehicle.

"I'm gonna text Sidney and get him to bring the minisub to Rick's Café in Negril. Have you ever been cliff diving?" Phoebe said.

"No, why?" T. L. said.

"The idea is for you and me to jump off the cliff at Rick's Café and into the sea! The water is at least forty-five feet deep there," Phoebe said.

"Really?" T. L. said, concerned.

"Take a look in the package that I picked up at the MoBay airport," Phoebe said.

T. L. looked in the package and pulled out a Kata Ring and an old spiral notebook.

"Surprise! You can add this Kata Ring to your collection! I told you we needed to talk, Terry. Our fathers were great friends, both professors in Philadelphia, and were secretly studying aspects of the Kata legend. Sometimes I heard them talking and writing things in this book. They didn't know I was listening, and I thought it was your father's fairy tales he was relating. I figured I'd finally come to Kata Cove myself and ask about the legend, and that's why I'm here," Phoebe said.

He put the ring on his finger, opened the spiral notebook, and saw a drawing of a large gold bracelet. "It appears that Kata created a backup plan and weapon in case he was separated from the Iron Thorn. It's a long golden cuff-bracelet that you wear on your right forearm: the Brace of Powers! It's my theory that if anyone wears the Brace of Powers on their wrist, they can command the Iron Thorn as their own! It was probably made for one of Kata's warriors. Written in this book is how the Brace of Powers controls the Iron Thorn," Phoebe said.

T. L. pulled out the underwater picture of the Cauldron of Gold. In the background, they saw the Brace of Powers on a skeleton's wrist on a shipwreck. "Phoebe, we better find that Brace of Powers before our enemies do!" T. L. said.

"Gotcha," Phoebe said.

"I also have to worry about the police. They want to arrest me," T. L. lamented.

"Not when you show them this," Phoebe said. Phoebe pulled out a picture of the barrels of stolen Sharp Jamaican Coffee hidden away on Layton's yacht and gave it to T. L.

"Honored to be aboard, Captain Penn," T. L. said with a smile.

In her Jeep, Phoebe and T. L. were a few hundred feet ahead of Morgan Gritch in his limo. Phoebe's phone beeped with a message. "Good, this says Sidney will be at Rick's. Get ready to dive!" Phoebe said.

Chapter 19:

DERRING-DO
AT RICK'S CAFÉ

At Rick's Café in Negril, Gritch had followed Phoebe and T. L. to the famous cliffside restaurant. Phoebe and T. L. entered the crowded restaurant and head for the cliffs, disrobing as they ran. "I'll jump first and make sure the *Stingray* is coming! Wait for my signal, and then dive in!" Phoebe said.

Phoebe dove off the cliff into the sea. The crowd at Rick's Café began to laugh and cheer as Gritch arrived, speaking on a megaphone: "Who's coming to the Buccaneer and Pirate Pier Festival?"

A Rick's Café crowd member said, "We are! Give us flyers!"

Gritch ran to T. L. by the cliff and grabbed his arm. "Where ye going, warrior? Who wants to see a display of derring-do? A little old-fashioned buccaneer swordplay?" Gritch said. Gritch tossed T. L. a real sword. The crowd applauded.

Gritch shouted to the crowd, "Here is my opponent! Kata, the Jamaican warrior! The so-called Iron Thorn!" The crowd cheered for T. L. He advanced with a dramatic thrust and Gritch fell over a barstool. "It seems my opponent has had some training!" Gritch said.

A crowd guy shouted at Gritch, "He's gonna kick your butt!" The crowd laughed.

T. L. smiled at Gritch and beckoned him on. Gritch said to the crowd, "I have sailed the seven seas, and I've never been bested by my enemies, including this poorly dressed vagabond!"

The crowd grew silent in reaction to Gritch's insult. A guy in the crowd, encouraging T. L., said, "Hey, Kata, shut that guy up!"

"I got this! En garde!" T. L. said. T. L. and Gritch dueled masterfully. Gritch got the better of T. L. as their blades locked, and he was on his back with his head hanging over the cliff. Gritch whispered in T. L.'s ear as they struggled cheek to cheek. "When I run ye through, it's going to look like an accident! OK? I'll spare yah life, Privateer, if ya tell me where the Ashanti gold is! Now, your dad's land that he left for you? I want you to know that I'm gonna take good care of it when you're gone! I'll play with the little students and the teacher! Oh, sweet Imani, my little teacher! It's your choice!"

"I'm not going anywhere! I'm Kata, the Iron Thorn! I'll come get you, whether I'm alive or dead!" T. L. said. T. L. shoved and kicked him backward. When Gritch advanced again, T. L. sidestepped him and tripped him into a table laden with bowls of jerk chicken sauce. The crowd roared with laughter as Gritch struggled in the mess.

T. L. ran to the cliff and saw Phoebe waving him in. "Thank you, ladies and gentlemen! I am Kata, the Iron Thorn! Forever forward! Woyo!" T. L. said.

The crowd responded in unison, "Forever forward! Woyo!"

T. L. made a perfect swan dive into the sea.

Chapter 20:

IMANI KIDNAPPED

Back at the Kata Cove Airfield, Imani got out of her plane. Something was amiss, as there were no workers at the airfield. Imani saw two black SUVs parked by the airfield hangar. The SUV doors opened, and Layton Lafontant and his bad-guy entourage got out. "Di hummingbird returns to her nest!" Layton said.

"Layton, what are you doing here? Where are my airfield workers?" Imani said.

"I paid dem to take a break, OK?" Layton thundered.

Thirty minutes later, on Layton's yacht, Imani wiped away tears as she was fitted into a pirate dress by Mia Gettens in Layton's bedroom. Mia was wearing Imani's mother's stolen diamond necklace. There was another tough-looking woman named Nancy wearing Empress Iyadola's stolen necklace and wristband and guarding the door. Imani noticed her phone in Layton's jacket hanging on the bedpost. She also saw her Kesi Gibson designer handbag on the bed and the Magic Golden Abeng hanging on a coat hook on the wall.

"Oh, stop ya cryin', Imani, it's betta dat Layton kidnapped you! Ya safer here dan ya are out dere! Di police are lookin' for ya cause ya stole ya modda's necklace to sell it fa money fa Terry Love!" Mia said.

"That's a lie, and you better give that back, Mia!" Imani said.

"Ya shut ya mout, girly!" Nancy said to Imani.

Imani saw a mongoose running into a corner hole. "Whoa! Did you see that? A mongoose!" Imani said.

"Ya teach in dat beat-up school at Kata Cove; ya scared of a little mouse?" Mia said.

"That was no mouse; that was a wild mongoose on a multimillion-dollar yacht!" Imani said.

"Layton came in with some mysterious cargo. Dey put it in di bottom of di yacht," Mia said.

"What kind of mysterious cargo? Di mongoose likes to eat coffee beans!" Imani said.

"So I don't ask questions! Best dat ya don't either! Ya can fix ya own dress!" Mia said.

Mia and Nancy stormed out of the room and locked the door behind them. Imani ran to Layton's jacket and took her phone out of its pocket. She turned it on and went into the bathroom to check it.

In the bathroom, Imani overheard Layton and one of his boat bad guys talking on the yacht deck. "Don't laugh! Der is a witch name Lady Crawlene. She used to be on our side, but we pissed her off!" Layton said.

"Oh no!" the boat bad guy said.

"Don't worry; Mi sent Gritch to do away wit her immediately! And dat Terry guy, mi got to get rid of him too! Gritch said dat Terry is back in Kata Cove!" Layton said.

"Dat ah hard mon for dead!" the boat bad guy said.

"A true dat! Anyway, maybe we'll find di Iron Thorn down in di sea too."

Layton laughed.

"Don't laugh, Mon. Mi hear dat di Iron Thorn is a real deadly weapon! Ya don't want ta mess wit dat Thorn, mon!" the boat bad guy said.

"Why not? I'll start a deadly sword collection," Layton said.

"Bwoy, mi hear di Kata legend from mi gran-folks! Dem told mi dat di Iron Thorn killed Kata way back when!" the boat bad guy said.

"Wha'? Mi nah hear dat one!" Layton said.

"Ya, mon, kill Kata dead! Got Kata right in di back!" the boat bad guy said.

"Whoa! Ah, backstab? Dat's tragic, mon!" Layton said. Layton and the boat bad guy jokingly performed a Kata fist-and-thumb bump. "Fo-fo!" Layton and the bad boat guy said. They both laughed mockingly.

In the bathroom, Imani was dismayed to hear that the Iron Thorn had killed Kata. She left the bathroom and looked at her phone, which indicated that she had missed eighty calls. Her phone rang, and she quietly answered. "Hello?" Imani said.

At the Barrett House, Uncle Wilvo was calling Imani on the phone, while the other Thorn Defenders and Mr. Sharp talked by the well. "Hello? Imani?" Uncle Wilvo said.

"Yes, Uncle Wilvo? I was about to call you!" Imani said.

"Thank God! Your father is here. Everyone is looking for you, and where is Terry Lee?" Uncle Wilvo said.

"I heard he might be back in Kata Cove. Listen, I can't talk long. I want to know something about the Kata legend. Uncle Wilvo, did the Iron Thorn kill Kata?" Imani said.

There was silence at the other end of the phone. "Hello, Uncle Wilvo?" Imani said.

"Where did you hear dat?" Uncle Wilvo said.

"Why, did it kill him?" Imani said.

Uncle Wilvo told Imani the bad news about the Kata legend. "As di legend goes, Empress Iyadola was kidnapped, taken to a pirate ship, and chained to di stolen Cauldron of Gold. Later, Kata and some of his warriors swam out to the pirate ship and searched it. Kata didn't know dat Empress Iyadola had di magic necklace and dat it had returned her safely to the beach at Kata Cove. Di only ting Kata saw was Empress Iyadola's crown of red hibiscus flowers floating in di water and thought the pirates had killed her. Kata's rage was out of control! He ordered di Iron Thorn to destroy every man and beast on board! He was in such agony dat he never commanded di Iron Thorn to stop killing and destroying. Imani, Kata died as di Iron Thorn took his life as well! *Yes, Imani, the Iron Thorn killed Kata!* Di ships sank to di bottom of di sea at Kata Cove as a result of the Iron Thorn's ferocity! Dat's where Kata is buried. He was so in love, Imani," Uncle Wilvo said.

Imani was in tears. "Yes. Oh, yes, he loved Empress Iyadola," Imani said.

"You've always said dat di Kata legend was like di Jamaican version of *Romeo and Juliet*," Uncle Wilvo said.

"Worse than *Romeo and Juliet*," Imani said.

"It is. However, dat sword is extremely dangerous! Dat's why we have to find Terry Lee now!" Uncle Wilvo said.

Imani heard Layton opening the door. She hung up the phone and put it behind her back as Layton entered. "No, no, don't speak! Don't deny mi what mi want for you. Mi gwan to change into something more appropriate for our evenin' togetha," Layton said.

Layton opened his closet, picked out a robe, went into the bathroom, closed the door, and started the shower. Imani set a giant rat trap in front of the bathroom door. She took a can of mosquito bomb from the shelf and activated it, producing a great deal of smoke. She spoke into an intercom unit that was on the wall. "Di yacht is on fire, everyone off di yacht now! Run for your lives!" Imani said.

People were running off the yacht, and Imani joined the escaping boarders. Mia and Nancy saw Imani escaping. Layton came out of the bathroom and realized that the so-called fire was a mosquito bomb. He also got his toe trapped. He spoke into the intercom. "We have a breach of security! All hands on deck, code red! Code red! Find Imani Sharp and return her to mi immediately! Ow!" Layton said.

Imani saw a Jet Ski at the side of the yacht but was confronted by Mia and Nancy. "Here she is! Stop her!" Mia said. Imani grabbed a sturdy mop. Imani hit Nancy over the head, knocking her down, and grabbed Empress Iyadola's necklace off Nancy's neck. Mia jumped on Imani's back. Imani snatched her mother's diamond necklace off Mia's neck and then flipped Mia into the water.

"Cool off!" Imani said. Layton's men surrounded Imani. Layton walked forward and stood in front of her.

"Gal, ya fightin' ah battle ya cyan't win!" Layton exclaimed.

Suddenly, Empress Iyadola's necklace started to pulsate with light, and Imani disappeared right before the bad guy's eyes. Imani reappeared on the Jet Ski, and she sped off.

Chapter 21:

NAN, DI QUEEN ENCHANTRESS

Meanwhile, at Lady Crawlene's lair, Lady Crawlene, Kriplin, and the three other duppies were having a meeting. Cats were chasing Monty, the pig. The Iron Thorn was lying in the middle of a table. A booming voice was suddenly heard. "Lady Crawlene Sands, prepare for a visit from Nan, di Queen Enchantress!" the booming voice said.

Crawlene was shocked and put a blanket over the Iron Thorn. Lady Crawlene told the duppies, "Disappear!" They quickly did.

Three floating and translucent older duppies appeared in front of a nervous Crawlene. In the center of the trio was the regal Queen Enchantress, now a duppy ghost. "Queen Enchantress and friends, dis is a surprise!" Lady Crawlene said.

"Surprise? Lady Crawlene, we expected ta hear from yu 'bout Kata's descendant's return! Wha' yu say him name was again?" Nan, di Queen Enchantress, said.

"Oh, yes, Terry Lee Barrett?" Lady Crawlene said.

"Yes. Dat's why yu return ta Kata Cove ta prepare an introduction wit Mr. Barrett an' us today! On dis great Kata's Celebration Day!" Nan, di Queen Enchantress, said.

"Queen Enchantress, Barrett was here, but it turns out dat him didn't know anyting 'bout Kata. Everyone laff at him, an' him left di island. Ran off scared! Ha!" Lady Crawlene said.

Nan, di Queen Enchantress, looked at Crawlene suspiciously. "Who scare off di descendant of our greatest warrior, an unda ya watch, Lady Crawlene? So, how could yu let dat happen, wit all ya supernatural powers? Ya essential job was ta help him adjust! Correct?" Nan, di Queen Enchantress, said. Crawlene looked down, ashamed.

Crawlene's parrots flew through the window and landed on her shoulders and whispered in her ear. "Mi parrots say Barrett is on him way back to Kata Cove!" Lady Crawlene beamed.

"Good, good! Now, we are goin' ta Kata Cove to pray for Kata's spirit. Will ya join us?" Nan, di Queen Enchantress, said.

"Of course, Queen Enchantress. Mi gwan feed mi animals, an' mi be right dere!" Lady Crawlene announced.

"OK, till lata', den," Nan, di Queen Enchantress, said.

Nan, di Queen Enchantress, and her entourage disappeared. Crawlene collapsed on the couch, relieved that they were gone.

Chapter 22:

IMANI OVERBOARD

M eanwhile, the Explorer ship was in the middle of Kata Cove. Maria and Barbara were watching a live, underwater video of the minisub with T. L., Phoebe, and Sidney returning from Montego Bay. "You guys are looking good! Prepare to dock!" Maria said on a walkie-talkie.

Maria and Barbara heard a voice out at sea. They went shipside and saw Imani slumped over and floating on the Jet Ski. "Imani!" Maria said.

"I ran out of gas!" Imani said.

"Oh my God! Hold on, Imani!" Barbara said. Maria threw Imani a life preserver with a rope attached, and Barbara dove into the sea and swam to Imani.

T. L., Phoebe, and Sidney surfaced the *Stingray* and saw Barbara and Maria helping Imani out of the water. They pulled the *Stingray* alongside the ship, and T. L. jumped on the ship. They laid Imani on a folding lounge chair. Ska-Bot brought Imani some hot tea, and she nursed the drink in the chair. "Oh, Imani, I'm so sorry." T. L. handed Imani the picture of the stolen barrels of Sharp Jamaican Coffee in the hold of Layton's yacht.

"I thought so," Imani concluded.

"I guess you've had enough of this spooky pirate adventure. We're going to get you back on land ASAP! Can I join you as soon as I get something called the Brace of Powers from the bottom of Kata Cove?" T. L. said.

"I'm feeling better, and you know what I want you to do?" Imani said.

"What's that, sweetheart?" T. L. said.

"Find the Brace of Powers and whatever else you need to find! Fo-fo, Kata!" Imani said.

T. L. and Imani did a Kata thumb-and-fist bump and hug.

Chapter 23:

GRITCH IS A GRINCH

Meanwhile, Lady Crawlene was looking at herself in the mirror, dressed up and prepared to go to Kata Cove. She heard and saw Morgan Gritch in his limo pull up to the front of her lair. Gritch walked into the house. "Lady Crawlene! I've been practicing our incantation for when we bring up and activate the Cauldron of Gold tomorrow! Here goes: 'Cauldron of Gold, awaken! Bring forth di Evil Ting!' How's that, witch?" Gritch exclaimed.

"Doesn't anyone knock anymore? And stop jokin' 'bout di Evil Ting!" Lady Crawlene said. Gritch was shocked to see the Iron Thorn lying in the middle of Crawlene's table. "What is this? The Iron Thorn? You were supposed to contact me as soon as it was found!" Gritch said.

"Oh, shut up! Who in di blazes are you! Mi been tryin to figure out how to get dis darn sword fa forty years!" Lady Crawlene said.

"Can you get it to fly?" Gritch said.

"Mi have worked many spells an' potions 'pon it, but it appears dat di original Kata had more power in him little finger dan all di sorcerers an' witches on dis island put togetha! Di only way mi can make di sword work is if mi wear di Brace of Powers! An' mi will need dat book!" Lady Crawlene pondered.

"The Brace of Powers and a book? What's that?" Gritch said.

"Listen, yu an' Layton Lafontant are tryin to cut mi out of di deal! Mi know dat! Mi nah work wit ya no more! Now, you know dat! Mi will not let either of ya losers get hold of dese treasures! Mr. Barrett is di rightful owna, but him too stupid to understan' dese treasures' powas, an' him cyan't be in charge a dem!" Lady Crawlene said.

Gritch quickly changed his mood and produced money. "Lady Crawlene, I have brought you a gratuity for your services. See, American tender!" Gritch said. Gritch tossed Crawlene a roll of US bills.

"Wha' ya tink ya gwan do? Gwan bribe mi? It is mi who bribe yu, circus mon!" Lady Crawlene said. Crawlene threw half the bag of the stolen Ashanti gold on the table, and the gold spilled out.

"By the power of Merlin, is that the Ashanti gold, Lady Crawlene?" Gritch said.

"Half of it!" Crawlene showed him the other half of the Ashanti gold in another bag in her hand.

"Ya make mi ah laugh! But ya good at makin' people laugh, bein' a clown!" Lady Crawlene said.

"Oh, curse you!" Gritch said.

Lady Crawlene laughed. "Yeh, likkle mon, a clown! Look, see here?" Lady Crawlene said. Crawlene showed Gritch an old picture of him in a clown suit in an English circus. "Ya come from a circus family from England! Ya whole family are clowns! Dey sent ya to Jamaica so ya Uncle Venables could teach ya some mannas, but ya nah learn nottin'!" Lady Crawlene mocked.

"I came to this island on my own accord for personal reasons, which you're too ignorant to understand! Enough of your insults, you old crow! What about the Brace of Powers and the book that you speak of?" Gritch demands.

"Ah, who ya call ol' crow? Mi gwan turn ya into a crow!" Lady Crawlene said.

Crawlene waved her hands in the air and zapped Gritch into a crow. The Gritch-Crow cawed, and then it began to inflate like a balloon. The Gritch-Crow exploded, with feathers flying, and Gritch reappeared, returned to his usual self. Gritch reached into his pocket and produced a mystical-looking crystal. "Crystal of Neahtid, a powerful force against witches, spells. Very useful, wouldn't ye say, obeah witch! Ha, ha, ha!" Gritch cackled.

Crawlene stared at Gritch, shocked. Gritch crushed the crystal in his hand and blew the crystal dust in Lady Crawlene's face, temporarily blinding her, and she fell to her knees. Gritch picked up the other bag of Ashanti gold now on the floor and put it in his pocket. Kriplin entered through the door wearing his raincoat. "Let 'er alone, you twit!" Kriplin said.

Kriplin scared Gritch, and he stumbled back. "Oh, it's you Kriplin, you ugly wanker. Say, matey, isn't it bloody hot in the Jamaican sun for ya?" Gritch said.

"Yes, that's why I have to wear this raincoat and hoodie to protect my sensitive skin," Kriplin said.

"Kriplin, do ye know who and what ye are?" Gritch said.

"What?" Kriplin asked.

"You were the first mate on a pirate ship in the seventeenth century that got bitten by a soucouyant!"

"A sou-cou…what's that?" Kriplin asked.

"Well, it's like a vampire, but from the Caribbean, which makes you a vampire anyway."

"Am I? Well, that would explain a lot," Kriplin said.

"Your boss, Lady Crawlene, never explained it to you, and you're an idiot because she put a forget spell on you."

Gritch quickly produced a garland of garlic and wrapped it around Kriplin's neck. "Jamaican garlic, quite rare and quite deadly for you," Gritch said.

Kriplin fell to his knees, choking. "Aaargh!"

Gritch grabbed the Iron Thorn and the other bag of Ashanti gold from the table. He pointed the Thorn behind Crawlene's head. "What of this Brace of Powers and the book?" Gritch said.

"Terry Love and Phoebe will be at Kata Cove. Dey will have di Brace of Powers and di book. So say mi parrots," Lady Crawlene said in tears.

"Thank you. Now was that so hard, obeah witch?" Gritch said.

Gritch raised the sword to do away with Crawlene, but the three other duppies entered the house, scaring him. Gritch ran to his limo with the Iron Thorn and the bags of Ashanti gold.

Chapter 24:

THE BUCCANEER AND PIRATE PIER FESTIVAL

The Buccaneer and Pirate Festival Day arrived. The whole parish and tourists were partying at Buccaneer and Pirate Pier. A band called the Kingston Ghouls was playing the classic reggae song "Pressure Drop," by Toots and the Maytals, on the main stage. The tethered helium tour balloon had parents and children in the basket and was slowly rising in the air by a balloon operator. There was a line of waiting balloon riders, including Marcus and Louise, the two children from Imani's class dressed up like Kata and Empress Iyadola.

"Now look, here they come! Di parade of buccaneer and pirate ships!" the announcer declared. The crowd cheered and ran to the coastline. Layton and his modern-day pirates were sailing in a procession of pirate flag–adorned ships in single file.

"Dis is excellent! Everyone is here as planned! Di whole parish!" Layton said.

"Everybody?" the boat bad guy said.

"Ya mean Imani Sharp? She jumped on a Jet Ski wit hardly any gas in it! Di sharks have probably neva' eatin' betta!" Layton said. All the modern-day pirates laughed.

Gritch rode up to the side of Layton's yacht on a Jet Ski with the Iron Thorn on his back. "Can we parley?" Gritch said.

"Gritch, you hornswaggla', where have ya been? No one's fed ya to the fish yet?" Layton said. Layton and the pirates helped Gritch on board the yacht. "Did ya do away wit Lady Crawlene?" Layton said.

"She is the least of my concerns now! Look at the powerful booty I've stolen!" Gritch said. Everyone moved back at the sight of the Iron Thorn. "With this, we can rule the world!" Gritch said.

All the modern-day pirates laughed.

"Fools! I'll show ye all when we get to Kata Cove!" Gritch said.

Layton pulled out his phone and called the helium tour balloon operator. "Shut down di balloon till we return!" Layton said.

The balloon operator stood at attention. "Aye, aye, Captain! Sorry, di balloon's closed!" the balloon operator said to the patrons. The kids and parents complained. A kid wearing a pirate costume grabbed the toy Iron Thorn out of Marcus's hand. A fight over the sword ensued. Layton's crew of miscreants headed to Kata Cove.

"To Kata Cove!" Layton said.

Chapter 25:

TAKEN HOSTAGE

Meanwhile, Dr. Liang, Dr. Venables, Taino, and Dreadlock Berky helped Uncle Wilvo into a fishing dingy on the beach at Kata Cove. "Do we have everything?" Dr. Liang said.

Uncle Wilvo looked at items in a burlap bag, including Kata's Golden Sledgehammer and his African crown and vest. "Yes!" Uncle Wilvo confirmed. They started the motor and drove out to sea.

Meanwhile, T. L., Phoebe, and Sidney were diving in the pirate ship graveyard at the bottom of Kata Cove, searching for the Brace of Powers. They passed by the Cauldron of Gold. "This must have been a gruesome battle," Phoebe said.

"Battle? More like a massacre! There's got to be more to this battle than we know. What would have made all these ships sink at the same time?" T. L. said.

The sub's equipment heat indicator started flashing red. "We're getting hot!" Sidney said. On a ship's mast rested the skeleton of the unfortunate pirate wearing the Brace of Powers.

"There it is!" T. L. said. Sidney operated a mechanical arm and grabbed the Brace of Powers. He pulled it into the sub hatch. Suddenly, the mast of the ship crumbled and fell on the minisub, trapping it on the seafloor.

Sharks began to circle the minisub. Phoebe and Sidney remained calm, while T. L. was beside himself.

"As soon as one of those sharks bumps that mast—" Phoebe said.

"I gotta tell you guys something!" T. L. said.

"What's that?" Phoebe and Sidney said.

"My father told me to destroy the Iron Thorn!" T. L. said.

"And you didn't? When did he tell you that?" Phoebe asked.

"Yesterday! I saw his ghost, and he told me," T. L. said.

"You saw his ghost, or did he look like he was alive?" Sidney said.

"He looked real, but he passed away years ago," T. L. said.

"If your father has passed away, but he still looks like he's alive, then your dad's a duppy, Terry! If he's a duppy ghost, he's got some unresolved issue dat he wants to fix! Or he wants *you* to fix! Like destroying di Iron Thorn!" Sidney said.

"Why didn't he destroy it himself?" T. L. said.

"He was too close to it! It meant too much to him! Remember, our ancestors, our parents, aren't perfect, Terry. We all have to improve on their lives, try to make the world a better place, as best we can!" Phoebe said. A shark bumped the mast, freeing the minisub, and they sped to the sea surface.

As the minisub surfaced, T. L., Phoebe, and Sidney saw the faces of Morgan Gritch and the modern-day pirates looking at them from over the side of Layton's yacht. The Cauldron of Gold was brought out of the sea and lowered to a platform on the crane ship by Layton's men. T. L., Imani, Taino, Phoebe, Sidney, Dreadlock Berky, Maria, Barbara, and the Iron Thorn Defenders were now hostages. "Bind and gag Barrett! Hold him down and search him!" Gritch said.

The modern-day pirates bound, gagged, and searched T. L. They gave Gritch the Brace of Powers and the book. Gritch put on the Brace of Powers and leafed through the book, wide-eyed. "We are wastin' precious time here, Gritch! Wha' gives?" Layton said.

"Now, let us see who the real Kata is!" Gritch said. Gritch took the Iron Thorn and tossed it in the air.

"Iron Thorn, mi command you to mi hand!" Gritch said. The sword responded and flew into his hand. He pointed the sword at the bad guy named Face. "Iron Thorn, mi command you to nyaka-nyaka Face!" Gritch said.

The sword leaped from Gritch's hands and stabbed Face in the shoulder, sending him over the side of the ship. "Good riddance! Wow! Gritch, dis is sometin' amazin'!" Layton said.

"Iron Thorn, mi command you to cease and sekkle! Iron Thorn, mi command you to mi hand!" Gritch said. The now-bloody Iron Thorn returned to Gritch's hand.

"Under me command, this sword will now be known as the Flyin' Iron Thorn!" Gritch said. Gritch pointed the Iron Thorn at Layton. "You repeat what I said!" Gritch said.

"Wha'? Di Flyin' Iron Thorn, mon!" Layton said.

"Listen, you! While you've been partying and wasting time with women and rum, I have been studying to be a wizard, conferring with the great minds of seventeenth-century alchemists. Why would an accomplished man like me hang out with fools like you? See here? I have rare Ashanti gold in my hand. Ashanti gold was brought to Jamaica by Kata and his warriors in the 1650s from the Gold Coast of Africa. When this rare gold is placed in the cauldron, it will create a potent potion, and when I drink it, it will make me the most powerful man in the world!" Gritch said.

"OK, Gritch, nuff talk. It's time for us to get out of here." Layton said.

"You are a hostage, Layton! You line up with the rest of the hostages." Gritch said.

"Boy, you have dishonored our family to no end. You will be scorned wherever you go. 'All You Need Is Love,' Morgan! Don't you get it?" Dr. Venables said.

"I did like that song. But no, Uncle Ven, I need more than a song! I need power! You're the disgrace to the family, living here among these vermin all your life! To you, I shall give no quarter! Resistance means death!" Gritch stated.

"Vermin? Who ya call vermin, Gritch?" Imani said with a defiant glare.

"Little Imani, you dare speak to me that way under these circumstances? I can only imagine what the next command will do!" Gritch said. Gritch looked at the brace and studied the next command from the book. He pointed the Iron Thorn toward Imani. He stated the following command: "Soro!" Suddenly, Gritch was propelled straight up into the air by the Brace of Powers.

"*Soro* is an African word for 'up,' " Uncle Wilvo said to T. L.

Gritch got stuck in the phony wooden crow's nest basket next to the fat, plastic pirate skeleton sticking out of it. He accidentally knocked the Brace of Powers off his wrist, and it fell into the sea, rendering him powerless. Gritch saw the Iron Thorn speeding straight for him. "Iron Thorn, mi command you to cease and—" Gritch screamed. The Iron Thorn stabbed Gritch in the heart, and its force launched Gritch out of the wooden crow's nest and into the sea; both Gritch and the Iron Thorn sank to the seafloor.

Back on the ship, T. L. removed his gag. "Let's get our sword back!" T. L. said.

Uncle Wilvo put his hand over T. L.'s mouth. "You need to sit down!" Uncle Wilvo said.

"Huh?" T. L. said.

"You should have destroyed di sword when you had di chance!" Uncle Wilvo said.

Dark clouds gathered, winds blew, and lightning flashed. "Are we ready?" Uncle Wilvo said. The Thorn Defenders spread their ceremonial items on an African rug, including Kata's original sledgehammer. "By the way, Terry, this Kata Ring is for you! I thought you should have it!" Dr. Liang said.

"I, too, would like to award you this essential Kata Ring. Good luck!" Dr. Venables said.

"What's going on?" T. L. whispered to Taino.

"You're asking di wrong scared person! Best close your eyes!" Taino said.

Chapter 26:

DI KATA RETURNS

O n the seafloor, Kata's skeleton, next to where a dead Morgan Gritch now rested, grabbed the Iron Thorn and the Brace of Powers. Kata rose out of the sea in his original human form and was furious. A ball of fire emanated from the Iron Thorn and blew one of Layton's pirate ships to smithereens. Kata flew to Layton's yacht and landed on the deck with his signature superhero pose: One-Knee-Down, Thorn-In-Di-Ground!

"*By di power of Nyankopon, di Kata has returned! FOREVAH FARWARD! Woyo!*" Kata said in a loud, booming voice.

"*FOREVAH FARWARD! Woyo! Wo, wo!*" the Iron Thorn Defenders said.

Frightened, T. L. placed his hand on the sledgehammer. "Don't even tink about it!" Uncle Wilvo warned.

The Thorn Defenders ran to Kata and cautiously placed his crown and vest on him. "Hail, Kata! Almighty warrior!" the Thorn Defenders said.

"Wah gwan!" Kata said. "Let us chant di African spirit libation proverb! It means dere is no bypass to God's destiny!" Uncle Wilvo said.

Kata joined in the libation chant. "*Onyame nkrabea nni kwatibea! Onyame nkrabea nni kwatibea!*" the defenders and Kata said.

"Who spirit we pray fa?" Kata said.

"Why, it is your spirit we are praying for, Kata! For you!" Uncle Wilvo said.

Kata laughed in disbelief. Uncle Wilvo nudged T. L. to speak. "Um. Kata, O great warrior, you've been dead for over three hundred years! Did you know that?" T. L. said.

Kata got in T. L.'s face. "Ya dare fool wit di Kata?" Kata said.

Phoebe accidentally bumped a button on her phone, and Ska-Bot made a musical appearance on her high-tech ship. Ska-Bot was playing a song: "You pick him up, you lick him down. Him bounce right back. What a hard man for dead!"

Kata bopped to Ska-Bot's music and then pointed the Iron Thorn at it. "Nice music, but shut dat ting up, mon!" Kata said.

Phoebe pressed a button on her phone, and Ska-Bot shut down.

"Over tree hundred years? Why am I still here? Has mi spirit never left Kata Cove? Mi still holdin' on, holdin' on for mi Empress Iyadola," Kata said, tearing up.

"It's been many years, Kata," Uncle Wilvo said.

Kata saw the Jamaican flag flying high on the ships. "How is Jamaica?" Kata asked.

"Jamaica is its own island and nation now! Jamaica is free, and we try to live in peace!" Uncle Wilvo said.

"Peace? Di pirates are gwan?" Kata said. Kata glares at the petrified group of Layton's pirates.

"More or less; there will always be some pirates. But we have our own flag and our own government, run by Jamaicans!" Uncle Wilvo said.

"Ya have some equal rights! Dis is good! So no more need fa di Kata?" Kata said.

"Your name lives on in legend and great respect, Kata! You are our mightiest ancestor! You will always be cherished and praised!" T. L. said.

"Ya, mon. Dat's true," Kata said.

"Look, Kata! Terry Lee Barrett, your descendant, strong and proud!" Dr. Venables said. Kata looked at T. L. and raised his thumb and fist to him, expecting a thumb-and-fist bump. T. L. gave Kata the thumb-and-fist bump. Kata looked at Imani, who was wearing Iyodola's magic necklace and wristband.

"You have given her Iyodola's necklace and wristband!" Kata said. Kata forcefully held T. L.'s and Imani's hands together. "You must have many children! You must marry immediately! Di Kata approves!" Kata said.

T. L. and Imani hugged, and the Iron Thorn Defenders cheered. Imani whispered in T. L.'s ear. T. L. gestured to Kata to join him to the side. "Thanks for everything, Kata. I have to tell you that my father ordered me to destroy the Iron Thorn," T. L. said.

"What ya chat bout, mon?" Kata said.

"He said times have changed, Kata. War is not the answer..." T. L. said.

Chapter 27:

DI CAULDRON OF GOLD

There was an explosion on the crane ship. Lady Crawlene was on a platform next to the ten-foot-tall, ten-foot-wide Cauldron of Gold. She had activated it and was waving her hands over it while Kriplin stood guard. "Cauldron of Gold, awaken!" Lady Crawlene said. The cauldron began pulsating; its belly was a purple, swirling, bottomless tempest.

"You tink dis is over without mi? Come on! Kata, it's sad dat mi haf to welcome ya home while ya are a duppy ghost! Welcome non-di-less! However, ya are a duppy ghost dat needs to cross over into the spirit world where ya now belong! Mi, Lady Crawlene Sands, di livin' obeah queen, will take over di watch of di Cauldron of Gold and di Iron Thorn until mi death!" Lady Crawlene said.

"Which may not be long from now, obeah queen! And ya want to destroy di Iron Thorn wit dis, bout cha! Mi don't tink so, mon! Not with people like dis around!" Kata said to T. L.

"Mi will take care of these precious treasures for ya! Ya descendant is not capable, as he is neither ah sorcera nor ah obeah, mon!" Lady Crawlene said.

"Ya not ah sorcera?" Kata said to T. L.

"Uh, no, but I could start a museum?" T. L. said.

"A museum? Wha' dat?" Kata said.

"Dis cauldron was a present for ya wedding anniversary, but ya ended everyting before ya found out what it could do! Now, mi gwan show ya, if ya don't hand over di Iron Thorn an di Brace of Powers!" Lady Crawlene said.

Kata laughed. "Ya won't obey? As ya wish den!"

"Duppy ghost pirates of Kata Cove, bring di Iron Thorn and di Brace of Powers to mi!" Lady Crawlene said. The ferocious duppy ghost pirates, now bearing wings, flew out of the cauldron like giant bats. A duppified Morgan Gritch led them. The duppy ghost pirates attacked.

In the ensuing battle on Layton's yacht, everyone was fighting for their lives. T. L. grabbed a sword and beheaded a duppy pirate. The Iron Thorn Defenders showed accomplished sword skills, eliminating an onslaught. A duppy pirate was chasing Layton and one of his henchmen down the passageway. Layton grabbed the henchman and pushed him toward the duppy pirate. The henchman was tackled by the duppy pirate, and Layton escaped.

Imani was trapped in the yacht conference room by a duppy pirate who approached her with a sword and net. Imani grabbed the Magic Golden Abeng out of her bag and blew on it twice, and Blacka the alligator appeared. He knocked the duppy pirate across the room. The duppy pirate got back up and threw the net on Blacka. While Blacka struggled to free himself, the duppy pirate raised his sword to do Imani in. Imani raised her arm in fear of the force of the blade.

Suddenly the golden lion emblazoned on Empress Iyadola's wristband animated itself, leaped off the wristband, grew enlarged, and roared ferociously. The lion's sudden appearance scared both the duppy ghost pirate and Imani, and they both ran out of the room.

Hearing the lion roars from outside, T. L. was stunned. T. L. asked Dreadlock Berky, "Are there lions in Jamaica?"

Dreadlock Berky responded, "Yes, I, only one, Rasta!" as he put a Rastafarian-style military cap on his head and stood at attention.

More duppy ghost pirates crawled out of the cauldron, but Kata, with a double hold on the Iron Thorn, commanded it to wipe them all out. "Kata, di baba boooom shockalocka!" Kata commanded. In one fell swoop laden with fire and lightning, all the duppy ghost pirates were mowed down. There was silence, as all were stunned by the Iron Thorn's destructive power.

In the silence, the Iron Thorn Defenders raised their swords to the air and looked toward Kata in awestruck acknowledgment. Kata nodded to them. A few duppy ghost pirates poked their heads out of the cauldron but decided it was best not to come out, and they disappeared back inside.

"And now, so-called obeah queen, ya fate is sealed!" Kata said. Suddenly, Lady Crawlene saw Nan, di Queen Enchantress sitting on the crane ship's deck, smoking a pipe and glaring at her, frightening Crawlene. After all, if Nan was unhappy with her, she could banish Crawlene from being an obeah queen for life, and that's just the beginning of what she could do. Crawlene immediately changed her attitude.

"Wait, Kata, you got it all wrong! Ya might tink mi to be greedy, but mi not! Mi tryin' to protect di Thorn and ya legacy from di ignorant! Mi can prove it, Kata! If you spare mi life, mi will let ya see ya wife, ya precious Empress Iyadola again!" Lady Crawlene pleaded.

"Mi Empress Iyadola, mi Empress Iyadola, mi can see her now? Mi Empress Iyadola?" Kata said.

On the crane ship, there was a flash of light and suddenly a beautiful and translucent Empress Iyadola was rising out of the cauldron. Empress Iyadola floated across the water. Empress Iyadola and Kata embraced. "Kata, mi been waitin' so long for you! Why haven't ya crossed over to Asamando, the spirit world?" Empress Iyadola said.

"Yes, mi know now! Mi been waitin' too! Mi was trapped in di sea!" Kata said.

"It's time to go, Kata! Our time has passed here! Terry an' Imani will protect Kata Cove now. Please come wit mi," Empress Iyadola pleaded.

Kata, with renewed strength, stood tall next to Empress Iyadola. "Mi will go wit you, mi love," Kata said.

Kata turned to T. L. and handed him the Iron Thorn, four of his Kata Rings, and the Brace of Powers. "If ya have any problems, don't wait ta call on ya ancestas!" Kata said. Kata grabbed T. L. by the arm and whispered in T. L.'s ear.

Meanwhile, across the deck, Layton gathered what was left of his modern-day pirates. "When Kata leaves, it's business as usual," Layton said.

Kata shook T. L.'s hand. "Terry Lee, Imani, Iron Thorn Defenders, an Jamaica, farewell!" Kata said. Kata and Empress Iyadola faded into the light and disappeared.

"Two down!" Layton said to his gang.

On the crane ship, the undead Morgan Gritch knocked Kriplin out and pushed Crawlene into the cauldron. She disappeared into the cauldron's swirling, bottomless pit with a bloodcurdling cry. "Aaaauurrgh!" Lady Crawlene said.

The undead Gritch took the bag of Ashanti gold from his pocket and poured it into the cauldron. The Ashanti gold spun in a circle in the cauldron. "Yes, the Moof-Ka-Zoot! It's working!" Gritch said.

On Layton's yacht, T. L. looked at the Iron Thorn. "The Iron Thorn does attract the wrong kind of attention, doesn't it?" T. L. said to Uncle Wilvo.

"And for far too many years now. We will have to fight like dis forever as long as it's around," Uncle Wilvo said.

Layton grabbed Imani's arm. Empress Iyadola's necklace began to pulsate with light, and Imani disappeared, to Layton's shock. "Again?" Layton said.

On the crane ship, Imani reappeared right behind Morgan Gritch. In the cauldron, the Ashanti gold liquefied. Gritch scooped the magic liquid up in a goblet. *"Forward ever, backward never!"* Imani said.

Gritch turned around, shocked. "What's that? Who's there?" Gritch said. Imani pushed Gritch into the cauldron. Gritch fell in but hung onto the cauldron's lip with one hand and drank the magic liquid from the goblet with the other. He then snatched Empress Iyadola's necklace off Imani's neck. The necklace fell into the cauldron's abyss and disappeared.

"Cauldron of Gold, bring forth di Evil Ting!" Gritch said.

The Cauldron of Gold began to froth and boil, and a lavalike substance began to rise from its bottomless pit.

"Terry, help!" Imani screamed.

On Layton's yacht, T. L. heard Imani scream and saw her struggling with Gritch by the Cauldron. He commanded the Iron Thorn to cut the chains that were holding up the Cauldron. "Iron Thorn, mi command you to nyaka-nyaka the chains!" T. L. commands.

On the crane ship, the Iron Thorn cut the chains, and the cauldron rolled out of control, dragging chains along with it. Gritch disappeared into the cauldron. A chain wrapped around Imani's leg. The cauldron crashed into the sea, and it appeared that the chains and the cauldron would drag Imani to her death. Imani fainted as she entered the water.

Suddenly, a flying T. L. with the Iron Thorn cut her chain. T. L. grabbed Imani around her waist and flew her back to Layton's yacht, placing her in front of the Thorn Defenders.

Chapter 28:

DI EVIL GRITCH TING

At the bottom of the sea, the Cauldron of Gold was still pulsating. There was an even bigger explosion from the cauldron. A monstrous Cthulhu-like beast came out of the cauldron and rose out of the sea. It had a white, pimple-ridden, pulsating, rubbery blob of a body, with multiple scaly tentacles and claws on its hind and forefeet and long narrow wings on its back, and it was as tall as a skyscraper. It smelled gross, like an enormous dead rat. One of the tentacles had a head on it. The head had bleached-blond hair and a scaly bald spot on top of its head. It was the head of the di Evil Gritch Ting! It spoke with Morgan Gritch's voice. "I will have the Iron Thorn now, along with ye life, Privateer! I will have all ye lives! Ye insubordinate, inferior fools!" the Gritch Ting said.

All were huddled together, watching the giant Evil Gritch Ting in extreme fear.

Uncle Wilvo handed T. L. Kata's old sledgehammer. "You do remember what your father told you?" Uncle Wilvo said.

"He said that when the Iron Thorn is destroyed, its pursuers will fly away! But before you destroy the sword, pour the Ashanti gold that's in your pocket on the sword first! Except I don't have the Ashanti gold in my pocket anymore!" T. L. said.

"I still have my Ashanti gold!" Imani said.

With their hearts racing with fear, T. L. dropped the Iron Thorn on the deck, and Imani dumped her bag of Ashanti gold on the blade. *"It's di last ting to do!"* T. L. yelled. He raised Kata's sledgehammer and then brought it down hard on the Iron Thorn, crumbling it into pieces.

Dark smoke came out of the crushed Iron Thorn; then, a tall vulture duppy spirit rose out of it. "Thank ya, Kata, for finally releasin' mi spirit from di sword! Awoah, don't worry 'bout dis monsta, him just ugly! Mi take care ah dis Ting fa ya, and den mi gwan! By di way, Kata, mi name is not di Iron Thorn, mi name is Big John Crow!" the vulture spirit said in a Jamaican vulture accent.

The vulture spirit, along with the broken pieces of the Iron Thorn, flew to di Evil Gritch Ting. The Iron Thorn and the Ashanti gold pieces swirled around di Evil Ting, completely encasing it.

"What is the meaning of this? Unclaw me!" Gritch Ting said.

The vulture spirit jumped to lightspeed and disappeared with di Evil Gritch Ting. The thunderclouds disappeared, and it was a bright, sunshiny day again. "Apparently, Gritch nyaka-nyaka'ed di Moof-Ka-Zoot," T. L. said to Imani.

T. L. put his hands over his heart. "Well, Dad, as usual, you were right again."

Imani hugged T. L., and the Thorn Defenders, old and new, surrounded them. "Hail to di Kata!" the Thorn Defenders said.

Layton and his pirate gang walked up to T. L. "Ya all shut up now! No sword, no peace! Get it? Ya lost ya back up, Mon! Ya stupid akata ancestor destroyed mi expensive ship! Now, who's gonna pay for dat, Barrett? Where ya hidin' dat Ashanti gold?" Layton said.

"Layton, do you consider yourself a greedy person? Didn't you see what just happened here? The people want peace. Chill out!" T. L. said.

"And ya shall have ya peace, at di bottom of Kata Cove!" Layton said. Layton shoved T. L. against a wall.

"That's it, then?" T. L. said.

"Show mi di Ashanti gold, Barrett! It's di last ting for ya to do! Mi will count to tree!" Layton said.

"It's your funeral, coffee pirate, and I will count to tree too!" T. L. said.

"Wha'?" Layton hesitated.

T. L. clapped his hands three times. "One, two, tree!" T. L. forcefully raised his fist and thumb in the air and yelled, "Forever Forward, Kata, the Iron Thorn. Woyo!"

Dramatically, with a rumble of thunder and a gust of wind, the original Kata instantaneously reappeared behind a petrified Layton and his four-person pirate gang. Across the deck, Imani and a reappeared Empress Iyadola looked on. Kata stared intensely at T. L. and pointed his finger at him. "When ya gwan make a new sword?" Kata said abruptly.

"Isn't there a better way, after all we've been through, Kata?" T. L. said.

Kata realized that T. L. had a good point. "Yah, mon. Good tinkin'!" Kata yielded.

Layton and his pirate gang stood paralyzed. "Ya gwan learn to respeck di Kata, mon! R-E-S-P-E-C-K! Neva call ah mon ah bush animal!" Kata lectured.

"Kata, mi nah say dat!" a scared Layton replied. Kata turned Layton around and bopped him on the top of his head, sending him to the deck floor. T. L., now wearing all of Kata's rings, made a fist, and a bolt of energy came out of the rings and blew the other pirates across the deck. They sat up, woozy. Kata grabbed a long rope and tied it around Layton and his pirate gang. Kata twirled the five pirates around like a human hammer throw and threw them all back toward the Buccaneer and Pirate Pier Festival.

Chapter 29

YOU WIN, TERRY LOVE

O n the main stage, the Kingston Ghouls band was performing in front of the festival crowd. The band saw the tied-up Layton and his pirate gang flying toward them. The band members jumped from the stage as Layton and company crashed into the drum set, to the crowd's shock. A dazed Layton spoke into the microphone while he stumbled around the stage.

"Ya win, Terry Love, ya win! Ya have ya peace! And we won't call ya no more bad names!" Layton raised his thumb and fist. "Max respect, brodda! Forever forward, mon! Fo-fo!" Layton said. Layton fainted.

By the pirate tour balloon, kids dressed like pirates chased Marcus and Louise dressed like Kata and Empress Iyadola into the tour balloon basket. Marcus and Louise slammed the basket door shut to protect themselves. The kids dressed like pirates surrounded the basket and accidentally unhooked the tour balloon lock. The balloon and basket flew into the air at a fast speed, and it broke the wire tethered to the balloon and basket.

The festival crowd screamed and shouted as the balloon glided away. "Oh, no! Oh, my! Save them!" the festival crowd shouted. Marcus and Louise opened the basket door and realized their situation and screamed.

Back on Layton's yacht, Kata fist-bumped T. L. "Di mon call Layton know ya have di backup now! Supernatural backup!" Kata said. T. L. and Kata performed the Kata hand salute again while Imani and Empress Iyadola stared seriously at them. T. L. and Kata stared back.

"What?" T. L. and Kata said. T. L., Kata, Imani, and Empress Iyadola heard and saw the kids in the tour balloon basket flying out of control over their heads. "That's Louise and Marcus in that basket!" Imani screamed.

"Ya could have saved di children if ya had di Iron Thorn! Ya could have used it ta fly! Or ya can use di Brace of Powers to fly!" Kata said.

T. L. had the Brace of Powers on his wrist. "Soro!" T. L. said. T. L. flew off toward the out-of-control balloon but flew right past it, unable to control his speed. Kata turned invisible, flew up to T. L., grabbed him, and flew T. L. to the tourist balloon.

Empress Iyadola went invisible and did the same thing with Imani. They placed both T. L. and Imani in the basket, and then the invisible Kata and Empress Iyadola pulled the tourist balloon back to the Buccaneer and Pirate Festival, landing it safely by the main stage to the crowd's wild applause.

The original Kata and Empress Iyadola reappeared briefly behind T. L. and Imani. They smiled and waved to Louise and Marcus, to their shock and delight.

The festival crowd shouted in unison, "Hail to di Kata! Hail to di Kata!"

T. L. was handed a microphone and spoke to the crowd. "I have laid down the sword of war! Now, I, DJ Terry Love, the reigning Kata, the Iron Thorn take up the sword of the spirit of peace and love! I shall speak truth to power, and I will work endlessly to see love overcome hatred and to live in peace! From this day forward, Kata Cove and Buccaneer and Pirate Pier will celebrate one man!" T. L. said on the mic.

Imani grabbed the mic. "One man and one woman: Kata and Empress Iyadola," Imani said. The festival crowd cheered!

"What do we of Kata *and* Empress Iyadola Cove and Buccaneer and Pirate Pier say?" T. L. said on the mic.

There were shouts of approval from the crowd, as all were suddenly wearing Kata and Empress Iyadola crowns. "Hail to di Kata! Hail to Empress Iyadola! Hail to di Kata! Hail to Empress Iyadola!" the crowd shouted.

In the crowd, T. L. saw five duppies. They were Dr. Leonard E. Barrett Sr. and his wife, Theodora, and Nan, di Queen Enchantress, and her entourage. T. L. gave them a forward-pointing thumbs-up from the stage. They gave a forward-pointing thumbs-up back, then disappeared. T. L. dropped the microphone, and T. L. and Imani kissed.

Chapter 30:

IMANI AND T. L. GET MARRIED

T. L. and Imani's blissful kiss segued into the two kissing at their wedding on Kata Cove Beach. An exuberant gospel choir sings the song "Holy Is the Lord" as they ran up the hill through a gauntlet of well-wishers to the Barrett House. In the crowd, T. L. saw Jason Clarke and gave him a Kata fist bump. "Hey, Jason, I'm going to be a little late getting back to Philly. Why don't you open my club as the guest DJ for a while and play reggae music all night long! I'll set it all up, OK?" T. L. said.

"Oh, yes indeed, reggae soul brodda!" Jason said.

Imani and T. L. were stopped by what appeared to be a youthful, thirtysomething Lady Crawlene Sands. The young-looking Crawlene clapped her hands, and two hummingbirds flew out of a golden box and gently placed Empress Iyadola's magic necklace around Imani's neck. The crowd cheered and applauded.

The parrot Ackee and Salt looked on from a tree. "Dem hummingbirds are always stealin' di show!" Ackee said.

"Always, but what cyan yah do?" Ackee and Salt laughed.

Imani and T. L. embraced in the bedroom window in the Barrett House that looked out to sea at what was now Kata and Empress Iyadola

Cove. T. L. was wearing Kata's ten magic rings. "Imani, what other things can these rings do? I am confused; my father tells me to get rid of these weapons, but I need them to keep the peace. Right?" T. L. said.

"Terry Love, Empress Iyadola said to me, when there is an agreed peace, put your weapons away! Or better yet, like your father said, destroy them! These weapons can kill by accident, and dat's di problem!" Imani said.

"Yeah, you are probably right," T. L. said.

"Oh, Terry, your uncle Wilvo said that according to the Kata legend, something amazing happens when you make two fists and bang those rings together, but—" Imani said.

"What? Bang them together? You mean like this?" T. L. said. T. L. made two fists and almost banged the rings together, right before noticing his father and mother's picture on the wall. T. L. took off the Kata Rings. "Well, we may not want to know. But I am not running from my past! And thank God we are living in the present!" T. L. said.

T. L. hugged Imani, and they looked out at the moonlit Kata Cove. "Living in the present, and going into our fantastic, forever-forward future together. *In Kata and Empress Iyadola Cove, Jamaica!*" T. L. said. They gave each other a fist-and-thumb bump and a kiss.

THE END

AUTHOR BIOGRAPHY

Terry Lee Barrett was born in Kingston, Jamaica, and raised in Philadelphia, Pennsylvania. He is the son of the Reverend Dr. Leonard E. Barrett and Theodora Jackson-Barrett.

Mr. Barrett is an award-winning DJ, journalist, and radio personality. Barrett's on-air entertainment debut began as the youngest host on the all-talk-radio formatted WHAT-AM program in Philadelphia. There, he produced and hosted the "Express Yourself to Terry Lee Barrett" talk show.

In 1979, he produced "The Infinite Hourglass," an African-American History commercial series nominated for the CEBA Award. His work drew WDAS AM/FM Radio's attention, where he worked from 1980 to 1987 as a news reporter and producer of the legendary "Georgie Woods Talk Show."

Barrett started a "Video-to-Go" company, which created the "Video Hawk" cable show and highlighted an array of artists from Janet Jackson to the Third World reggae band.

Music was always Barrett's real love. He continued his rise on the entertainment and music scene by hosting the top-rated Caribbean/World Music Show, "Caribbean Rhythms" on WRTI FM, from 1987 to 1995. He produced, hosted, and emceed numerous live shows.

During this time, two Philadelphia building developers invited Barrett to an abandoned pier on the Philadelphia waterfront. They said they were going to build a club in honor of his show, and the legendary "Katmandu" Restaurant, Nightclub, and Marina was born. Barrett became the House DJ at this world-renowned world music hot spot for the next 12 years. A second Katmandu opened on the New Jersey waterfront, where Barrett also deejayed.

Barrett has worked at four radio stations in Philadelphia: WHAT AM, WDAS FM, WRTI FM, WKDU FM, and WMMR FM.

Now a screenwriter, Barrett is marketing his screenplays worldwide and has written his Caribbean epic screenplay entitled "Kata The Iron Thorn" in honor of his late father, the world-renowned anthropologist and author, the Reverend Dr. Leonard E. Barrett, Ph.D.